DEAD RECKONING

A Novel

By Del Wilber

Copyright Page

DEAD RECKONING

First Edition: September 2025
ISBN: 978-1-970330-07-6

Library of Congress Control Number:

Printed in the United States of America

10 9 8 7 6 5 4 3 2 1

9 781970 330076

Table of Contents

Chapter 1: Storm Watch

The barometer had been falling since dawn.

Elias Johnson felt it in his bones before he saw the brass needle trembling two points below yesterday's mark. Twenty-three years at sea had taught him to read the ocean's moods like scripture—the way the swells grew longer and more deliberate, how the wind backed from southwest to south-southeast, carrying with it the metallic taste of distant lightning.

"Mr. Johnson." Third Mate Hartwell appeared at his shoulder, voice tight with the particular strain that came from watching a storm build while the captain remained absent from deck. "The glass has dropped another point this past hour."

Elias nodded, not taking his eyes from the horizon where a bank of slate-gray clouds gathered like an advancing army. The merchant barque *Cassandra* rode easily enough for now, her cargo of Nova Scotia timber bound for Rio de Janeiro, but the sea was telling stories that made his sailor's instincts prickle.

"Have you seen Captain Morrison this morning?"

Hartwell's hesitation spoke volumes. "He... retired to his cabin after the noon sight, sir. Said he wasn't to be disturbed."

Retired. A polite word for what they all knew. Morrison had been drinking heavily since they'd cleared Halifax three days ago, nursing some private grief that had grown worse with each league southward. A good man once, perhaps, but the bottle had claimed him as surely as any reef.

The wind gusted, setting the rigging to singing a higher note, and Elias felt the first drops of moisture in the air. Not rain yet, but the promise of it.

"Mr. Hartwell, pass the word for all hands to secure for heavy weather. Double-lash the boats, see the hatches are properly battened, and check the lashings on that deck cargo forward."

"Aye, sir." Hartwell paused. "Should we not wake the captain?"

Before Elias could answer, Second Mate Brennan emerged from the companionway, his pale eyes taking in the darkening sky with something that might have been satisfaction. Thomas Brennan had sailed under Elias for two voyages now, competent enough in fair weather but possessed of an ambitious streak that ran deeper than the Mariana Trench.

"Bit of wind coming, is there?" Brennan's tone carried just enough insolence to skate the edge of insubordination. "Perhaps we should reduce sail before we alarm the passengers."

Passengers. They carried only cargo this voyage, but Brennan had a gift for making everything sound like a slight. Elias studied the man's face, noting the calculating gleam behind the deference.

"The passengers, Mr. Brennan, are safely stowed in the hold as timber," Elias said evenly. "As for reducing sail, we'll wait until we must. This blow may pass to the south of us yet."

"Of course, sir. You're the First Mate." Brennan's emphasis on the rank stung like a lash. "Though I wonder if Captain Morrison might have... different thoughts on the matter."

The crew had paused in their work, sensing the tension crackling between the officers like static before lightning. Elias felt their eyes upon him, measuring, weighing. In moments like these, authority hung by threads finer than spider silk.

"Mr. Brennan," Elias said quietly, "you'll see to the storm canvas. Have the storm trysail bent on and ready to hoist. We may have need of it before the day is done."

"I think not." Brennan's mask slipped entirely now, revealing the naked ambition beneath. "I've been watching this weather longer than you think, and it's naught but a summer squall. We've seen worse in the Bay of Fundy."

The barometer chose that moment to drop another point with an audible click, as if the very air had grown suddenly thin. A longer gust sent the ship heeling slightly to port, and somewhere in the rigging, a block began to rattle with increasing urgency.

Elias felt the moment crystallize around him like ice forming on a winter morning. Twenty men stood watching, the ship herself seemed to hold her breath, and in the captain's cabin below, Morrison likely lay in a stupor that rendered him less useful than ballast.

"Mr. Brennan," Elias said, his voice carrying the full weight of his authority, "you will see to the storm canvas, or you will see to your sea chest. The choice is yours."

For a heartbeat, Brennan's hand moved toward his pocket —where Elias knew he kept a small knife for cutting line —and the crew stirred uneasily. But then the man's eyes shifted, calculating odds, and he stepped back.

"As you wish, *sir.*" The word dripped with venom. "Though I'll note in the log that this was done against my counsel."

"Note what you like," Elias replied, already turning away. "Mr. Hartwell, take four good men and get those storm stays rigged. I want this ship ready for whatever that sky means to throw at us."

The wind rose another note, and the first real drops of rain began to spatter the deck like scattered coins.

"All hands!" Elias called, his voice carrying clear above the growing symphony of wind and rigging. "All hands to shorten sail!"

The storm struck with the sudden fury of a cannon broadside.

One moment the *Cassandra* was running easily under topsails and jib, the next she was buried rail-deep in green water as a wall of wind and rain swept across her decks. Elias had seen it coming in the final moments—a dark line racing across the water like cavalry at full charge—but even his shouted warnings barely reached the crew before the tempest was upon them.

"Clew up the main topsail!" he roared, but his voice was snatched away by the howling wind. The ship lurched violently to starboard, throwing two men hard against the bulwark, and Elias heard the ominous crack of straining timber somewhere in the rigging above.

Through the driving rain, he could see Hartwell forward, rallying the crew with gestures more than words, while Brennan had taken shelter behind the mizzen mast, making no effort to assist. The coward's true nature revealed itself when the sea showed teeth.

The fore topsail was flogging itself to ribbons, the canvas snapping like musket fire in the gale. If they didn't secure it soon, the sail would tear away completely, taking the yard and possibly the topmast with it. Elias looked for someone to send aloft, but every man was struggling just to keep his footing on the water-slicked deck.

"The fore topsail!" Hartwell appeared at his elbow, having to shout directly into his ear to be heard. "She'll shake herself to pieces!"

Elias nodded grimly. The standard procedure would be to send the most experienced topman up to secure the sail, but Davis, their best rigger, was forward battling to get the jib down, and young McCarthy was new enough to the trade that sending him aloft in these conditions would be tantamount to murder.

Another massive gust struck the ship, and the fore topsail gave an particularly violent crack. Elias saw a section of canvas tear away and whip into the darkness like a fleeing ghost. In minutes, they would lose the entire sail—and in these seas, that could spell disaster for them all.

"Take the deck," he told Hartwell, and before the Third Mate could protest, Elias was making his way forward, timing his movements to the ship's violent rolling.

The ratlines were slick with spray and rain, treacherous as ice. Elias paused at the futtock shrouds, feeling the familiar weight of responsibility settle on his shoulders like a mantle. He had not been aloft in a blow like this for three years, not since he'd made First Mate and could delegate such work to younger, more nimble hands. But tonight, with Morrison senseless below and Brennan proving worse than useless, the ship needed him to be more than just an officer giving orders.

She needed him to be a sailor.

The climb up through the lubber's hole would have been easier, but Elias chose the harder path over the futtock shrouds—partly from habit, partly because the men needed to see their First Mate do things the proper way. The wind tried to tear him loose with every step, and twice he had to pause as the ship rolled so far to starboard that he hung nearly horizontal, supported only by his grip on the tarred rope.

At the fore topsail yard, the situation was worse than he'd feared. The sail had torn along the bolt rope, and the loose canvas was threatening to wrap itself around the rigging. Working by feel more than sight in the howling darkness, Elias began the dangerous task of gathering the rebellious sailcloth, his hands quickly going numb in the cold and wet.

A particularly vicious gust nearly tore him from his perch, and for one heart-stopping moment he swung free, supported only by his death grip on a section of canvas. Below, he could see the white faces of the crew turned upward, watching their First Mate fight for his life sixty feet above the deck.

This is what Morrison should be doing, Elias thought grimly as he hauled himself back to the yard. *This is what command means.*

It took him twenty minutes to secure the torn topsail, lashing the canvas with gaskets until it lay quiet against the yard. By the time he descended to the deck, soaked through and exhausted, the worst of the squall was passing, leaving the *Cassandra* to ride more easily under storm canvas.

"Well done, Mr. Johnson," Hartwell said quietly, and there was something in the young officer's voice—a respect that had not been there before.

Elias looked around the deck, taking inventory. Two men had been injured but not seriously, the cargo appeared secure, and most importantly, the ship was intact and seaworthy. They had weathered the blow, though not without cost. He could see it in the faces of the crew— exhaustion, relief, and something else. Something that looked uncommonly like admiration.

Brennan emerged from his shelter, attempting to look as though he had been busy with important duties. "Bit of a blow," he said casually. "Nothing we couldn't handle, of course."

The crew's contemptuous looks spoke volumes about what they thought of their Second Mate's contribution to the evening's work. Elias said nothing, but filed the moment away for future reference. A man's true character always revealed itself when the sea turned ugly.

"Mr. Hartwell, secure from storm stations. Set the usual watches, and have the cook break out some hot coffee for the lads. They've earned it." Elias wiped rain from his eyes, suddenly feeling every one of his thirty-seven years. "I'll be in my cabin, working on the log."

The small cabin that served as Elias's quarters felt like a sanctuary after the violence of the storm. He hung his oilskins on their peg and lit the gimbal lamp, casting dancing shadows on the bulkheads as the ship continued her long roll through the subsiding seas. The familiar surroundings—his few books, the daguerreotype of his mother back in Yarmouth, the brass chronometer ticking steadily on its shelf—seemed to anchor him to something solid after the chaos above.

He pulled out the ship's log and dipped his pen, pausing to consider how to record the evening's events. The official version would be terse and professional: "Heavy squall from the SW, reduced sail, no significant damage." But as he began to write, his mind wandered to larger questions than maritime bookkeeping.

Twenty-three years. More than half his life spent learning the sea's lessons, climbing from ship's boy to First Mate through a combination of hard work, natural ability, and the kind of luck that kept good sailors alive while claiming the careless and unlucky. He remembered his first storm, twelve years old and terrified, clinging to the rigging of a fishing schooner off the Grand Banks while his father's friend shouted encouragement through the gale. "The sea don't care if you're scared, boy! She only cares if you do your job!"

That man had been right. The ocean was indifferent to human fears, ambitions, or politics. She tested you without regard to rank or reputation, and she measured your worth not in words but in actions. Tonight, when the *Cassandra* had needed someone to go aloft, the sea hadn't cared that he was First Mate, that his proper place was on deck giving orders. She had simply presented a problem that required solving, and either he was sailor enough to solve it, or he wasn't.

The knowledge that he was—that after all these years, he could still climb rigging in a gale and fight rebellious canvas into submission—filled him with a quiet satisfaction that had nothing to do with the crew's approval or Brennan's resentment.

He thought of his mother, waiting in their small house overlooking Yarmouth harbor. She would be sitting by the window as she did every evening, watching the ships come and go, hoping for news of her son. Margaret Johnson had raised him alone after his father's death, had watched him go to sea at fourteen with the stoic acceptance that was bred into Maritime women. She understood that the ocean was both provider and destroyer, that it gave men purpose but demanded payment in worry and loss.

"You have good sea sense, Elias," she had told him before this voyage. "Like your father. But remember—the sea doesn't owe you anything, no matter how well you know her ways."

Sound advice, as always. Tonight had reminded him that respect had to be earned anew with each storm, each crisis, each moment when seamanship mattered more than seniority. He had passed tonight's test, but there would be others. There always were.

A knock at his door interrupted his thoughts. "Come," he called, setting down his pen.

Hartwell stepped inside, ducking his head under the low beam. "Beg pardon, Mr. Johnson, but I wanted to thank you. For what you did tonight. The lads... well, they're talking about it."

Elias nodded, unsurprised. Word traveled fast on a ship, and by tomorrow morning every man aboard would know that their First Mate had gone aloft when the situation demanded it, while their Second Mate had found pressing business elsewhere.

"It needed doing," he said simply. "Ship comes first."

"Yes, sir. But still..." Hartwell paused, seeming to weigh his words carefully. "It's good to sail with officers who remember they're sailors too."

After the Third Mate left, Elias returned to his log entry, but found himself staring at the blank page instead of writing. *Officers who remember they're sailors too.* The phrase resonated more than Hartwell probably realized. In his years climbing through the ranks, Elias had served under captains who ruled through fear, others who commanded through competence, and a few who seemed to think that gold braid automatically conferred wisdom.

The best had been those who never forgot that the sea made its own rules, and rank meant nothing if you couldn't do your job when it mattered.

He dipped his pen again and wrote: "2200 hours - Heavy squall from SW. Reduced to storm canvas. Fore topsail damaged, secured aloft. Ship and crew in good order. Glass rising."

Simple, factual, professional. No mention of Morrison's absence, Brennan's cowardice, or his own climb through the storm-lashed rigging. The sea knew what had happened, and the crew knew, and in the end, that was enough.

Outside his porthole, the last of the storm clouds were breaking apart, revealing patches of star-studded sky. The *Cassandra* rode easier now, her motion settling into the familiar rhythm that had lulled generations of sailors to sleep. Tomorrow would bring new challenges—it always did. But tonight, ship and crew had faced the tempest and emerged intact.

For a sailor, that was victory enough.

Elias closed the log, extinguished the lamp, and settled into his narrow bunk. Through the bulkhead, he could hear the night watch moving about on deck, keeping their eternal vigil. The sound was comforting, a reminder that no matter what storms might come, good sailors would always answer the sea's call.

As he drifted toward sleep, he found himself thinking once more of his mother, and of the long journey that had brought him from ship's boy to First Mate. The path ahead remained uncertain—there would be other storms, other tests, other men like Brennan who confused ambition with ability. But tonight had reminded him of something important: he was still, at heart, what he had always been.

A sailor. And on a night like this, that was enough.

Chapter 2: Yarmouth Son

The morning after the storm dawned clear and bright, with the kind of crystalline air that made every line of rigging stand out sharp against the blue sky. Elias stood at the taffrail, watching the *Cassandra's* wake stretch away toward the northern horizon where, somewhere beyond the curve of the earth, Nova Scotia waited under its blanket of early autumn.

Yarmouth. Even the name carried the salt smell of home— the busy harbor crowded with vessels from every corner of the Maritime provinces, the forests of masts swaying like a winter woodland, the comfortable bustle of a town that lived and breathed by the sea's rhythm. It was a place where every family had someone before the mast, where the sound of shipyard hammers rang from dawn to dusk, and where widows' walks crowned half the houses like white wooden crowns.

His mother would be sitting in her kitchen now, he calculated, working on some piece of needlework while the morning light streamed through windows that faced the harbor. Margaret Johnson had spent thirty-two years watching ships come and go, first as a sailor's wife, then as a sailor's mother. She had learned to read the weather signs as well as any man, not from any love of the sea but from necessity—the knowledge that wind and wave ruled her family's fate as surely as they ruled the tides.

She had been barely eighteen when she married Duncan Johnson, a whaling man with laughing eyes and hands as steady as bedrock. Elias's earliest memories were fragments, bright pieces of a childhood that had ended too abruptly: his father's voice singing old chanties while he carved toy boats from driftwood, the smell of pipe tobacco and tar that clung to his sea clothes, the way he would hoist five-year-old Elias to his shoulders and point out the different rigs in the harbor.

"See there, laddie? That's a brigantine—two masts, square-rigged on the foremast, fore-and-aft on the main. And that beauty with all the canvas? Full-rigged ship, three masts, square sails on all of them. Finest sight on God's ocean when the wind's fair and she's running free."

The memories were precious partly because there were so few of them. Duncan Johnson had sailed on his last whaling voyage when Elias was five, bound for the Arctic grounds in the barque *Northern Star*. The ship had returned seven months later with a good catch of oil and bone, but without six of her crew—including the steady, laughing man who had taught his son to identify ships by their silhouettes.

Elias could still remember the day the news came. He had been playing in the small garden behind their house, building elaborate harbors in the dirt with his collection of wooden vessels, when his mother's voice had called him inside. Her face had been pale but composed, and she had knelt down to take his small hands in hers.

"Your father won't be coming home from this voyage, Elias," she had said, her voice steady despite the tears that ran silent tracks down her cheeks. "There was an accident with one of the boats. He... he's gone to be with the Lord."

The details had come later, filtered through the conversations of adults who thought he was too young to understand. A bull sperm whale had stove in Duncan's boat somewhere in the Davis Strait, taking him and two other men down in the frigid Arctic waters. The survivors had searched for hours, but the sea had claimed its due and given nothing back.

Margaret Johnson had faced widowhood with the quiet strength that seemed bred into Maritime women. There had been no dramatic collapse, no theatrical displays of grief—just the steady, daily business of survival. She had taken in sewing and washing, had sold her husband's few personal effects except for his sea chest and the daguerreotype that still sat on her mantelpiece. Most importantly, she had raised her son with the understanding that the sea, however cruel it might be, was still their livelihood.

"The ocean gives and the ocean takes," she had told him once, watching a funeral procession wind its way up from the harbor. "It's not good or evil, Elias—it just is. Like the weather, like the tides. A man can rage against it or he can learn to work with it, but he can't change it."

By the time Elias was twelve, it was clear that formal schooling held little attraction for him. He could read and cipher well enough, but his heart belonged to the harbor. He spent his free hours among the ships, learning the names of every line and sail, listening to the stories of old salts who remembered when Yarmouth's fleet had been the largest per capita in the world. The town's merchants and shipowners were legends in their own right—men who had built fortunes on timber and cod, who sent their vessels to every corner of the globe and brought back the exotic products that made Nova Scotia rich.

It was inevitable that he would go to sea. The only question had been when and on what terms.

"Fourteen's young," his mother had said when Captain Jeremiah Haliburton had offered to take the boy as ship's boy aboard the brig *Mary Catherine*. "But not too young. Your father was thirteen when he first went before the mast."

Elias remembered that conversation as clearly as if it had happened yesterday. They had been sitting in the small parlor, the same room where she had told him of his father's death nine years earlier. Captain Haliburton, a weathered man with kind eyes and a reputation for fairness, had laid out the terms: three years as ship's boy, learning every aspect of seamanship from the deck up. No wages the first year, small wages thereafter, but an education that no landsman's school could provide.

"The boy has the look of a sailor about him," Haliburton had said, studying Elias with the careful attention of a man who had learned to judge character quickly. "Good hands, steady nerves, and he's been around ships enough to know the difference between a halyard and a sheet. More importantly, he wants to learn. That's worth more than size or strength in a green hand."

Margaret had looked at her son for a long moment, seeing perhaps not the eager fourteen-year-old before her but the five-year-old who had built harbors in the dirt while his father sailed toward his death. But when she spoke, her voice was steady.

"If it's what you want, Elias, then it's what you'll do. But remember—going to sea isn't a game. The ocean doesn't care that you're young or that you miss your home. It'll test you every day, and some days you'll wonder why you ever left dry land."

She had been right, of course. That first voyage—six months to the West Indies and back with a cargo of salt fish—had been a brutal introduction to life before the mast. Elias had been seasick for a week, homesick for a month, and had seriously considered jumping ship in Barbados. But Captain Haliburton had been a good teacher, and the *Mary Catherine's* crew had taken the young Nova Scotian under their collective wing.

"Every sailor learns the same lessons," old Tom Webber, the bosun, had told him during one particularly miserable night watch. "How to hand, reef, and steer. How to splice and serve. How to read the sky and feel the wind. But most important, how to be part of something bigger than yourself. A ship's crew is like a family, boy—sometimes you love 'em, sometimes you want to throttle 'em, but you always look out for each other."

The lessons had taken root. By the end of his first year, Elias could lay aloft with the best of them, could tie every knot in the book blindfolded, and had learned to find his sea legs on anything from a flat calm to a full gale. More importantly, he had discovered that he possessed something that couldn't be taught—an instinctive feel for ships and the sea that marked the difference between a competent sailor and a natural seaman.

His second year had seen him promoted to ordinary seaman, his third to able seaman. When his indenture with Captain Haliburton ended, Elias had faced a choice that every ambitious sailor confronted: stay with a good berth where he was valued, or seek his fortune on larger ships with better opportunities for advancement.

He had chosen advancement, signing aboard the barque *Acadia* as an able seaman for a voyage to Liverpool and back. It was the beginning of a decade of careful career building, ship by ship, voyage by voyage. He had sailed on everything from coastal schooners to deep-water ships, had weathered hurricanes in the Caribbean and winter gales in the North Atlantic. He had served under captains who were tyrants and captains who were saints, had learned to navigate by sun and stars, had mastered the thousand small skills that separated professional seamen from mere sailors.

The turning point had come seven years ago, when he was twenty-nine and serving as second mate aboard the ship *Intrepid*. They had been bound from Saint John to London with a cargo of deals and timber when their captain had been stricken with appendicitis three days out. The first mate, a competent but unimaginative man named Fletcher, had found himself in command of a situation that rapidly deteriorated when they encountered a series of autumn gales.

Fletcher's hesitation in the face of crisis had nearly cost them the ship. It was Elias who had taken the initiative to get storm canvas on her, Elias who had organized the crew to pump her dry when she began taking water in the heavy seas, Elias who had navigated them safely into Cork when the damage made continuing to London impossible. The ship's owners, impressed by the reports they received, had offered him Fletcher's position when they reached port.

His first command as chief mate had been aboard the brig *Constellation*, running lumber to the West Indies. It was a small step up, but it had led to better berths—larger ships, more prestigious routes, higher wages. For eight years he had built his reputation voyage by voyage, earning the respect of crews and the confidence of owners who valued reliability above all else.

But it was always his mother's face he saw in his mind's eye when he signed the articles for a new voyage, her quiet strength that had shaped his understanding of duty and responsibility. She had never remarried, though she was still a handsome woman who drew the attention of Yarmouth's widowers and bachelors. When Elias had asked her about it once, she had simply smiled.

"One good man was enough for this lifetime," she had said. "Besides, someone has to be here when you come home."

Home. The word carried more weight now than it had when he was fourteen and eager to see the world. Elias understood now what his mother had always known—that home wasn't just a place you came from, but a place you carried with you. It was the knowledge that someone waited, that someone cared whether you returned safely from whatever distant waters called your name.

A step on the deck behind him interrupted his reverie. He turned to see Hartwell approaching with the morning's observations, the young officer's face showing the careful neutrality that meant business.

"Morning, Mr. Johnson. Noon sight puts us at thirty-eight degrees, fifteen minutes north. Making good speed on this heading—should raise the Azores day after tomorrow if this wind holds."

Elias nodded, accepting the slate with their position worked out in Hartwell's careful hand. "Very good, Mr. Hartwell. Any word from the captain this morning?"

"No, sir. Still... indisposed."

They both knew what that meant. Morrison's drinking had grown worse since the storm, if such a thing were possible. The man seemed to be wrestling with demons that no amount of rum could quiet, and Elias found himself effectively in command of the ship with two weeks still to run before they raised the Brazilian coast.

It was not an unprecedented situation—he had sailed with captains who drank, captains who were incompetent, captains who simply disappeared into their cabins and left the ship to run itself. But it was always a delicate balance, maintaining discipline and purpose when the man who should provide both was absent from the equation.

"Mr. Hartwell," he said finally, "see that the captain's meals are sent to his cabin as usual. And pass the word that I'll be taking the noon sight myself today."

"Aye, sir." Hartwell paused, then added quietly, "The men are talking, you know. About last night, about the captain. They look to you now."

Elias studied the young officer's earnest face, seeing in it something of his own younger self—the eager competence, the desire to do right by ship and crew, the gradual understanding that seamanship was as much about people as it was about wind and canvas.

"Let them talk," he said. "But make sure they understand that this ship has a captain, whatever his current... difficulties. Chain of command exists for good reasons,

Mr. Hartwell. The moment we forget that, we stop being a crew and become a mob."

It was a lesson his mother had taught him in different words: respect the order of things, even when that order seemed flawed. Duncan Johnson had died following orders from a boat steerer he had known was reckless, but he had never questioned the hierarchy that put that man in command of his boat. Some things were larger than individual judgment, more important than personal opinion.

As Hartwell headed forward to relay his orders, Elias turned back to his contemplation of the wake stretching away toward home. Two more weeks to Rio, then the return voyage with whatever cargo they could find—coffee, sugar, hides, perhaps some of the precious hardwoods that brought good prices in Nova Scotia's furniture shops. Another three months before he would see Yarmouth harbor again, before he could sit in his mother's kitchen and tell her about the storm, about Morrison's drinking, about the way the crew had looked at him when he came down from the rigging with the fore topsail secured.

She would listen without judgment, as she always did, and then she would ask the question that mattered most: "Did you do right by your ship and your men?"

The answer, Elias knew, would determine not just how he remembered this voyage, but how he faced the next one. The sea demanded many things of those who served her, but perhaps the most important was this: that you earn your place anew each day, that you prove yourself worthy of the trust placed in you by wind and wave and the men who depended on your judgment.

It was a lesson worth remembering, especially with Rio still two weeks away and Thomas Brennan watching every move he made with calculating eyes.

The *Cassandra* sailed on through the morning, her wake white and straight behind her, carrying twenty-three souls toward whatever the southern ocean had in store for them. And at her stern, the First Mate stood watch, thinking of home and the long road that had brought him to this moment of responsibility and command.

Chapter 3: Captain's Papers

The examination hall in Halifax smelled of salt air, old wood, and the particular brand of nervous sweat that came from men facing the most important test of their maritime careers. Elias sat at one of the scarred wooden tables, his master's examination papers spread before him like battle plans, while outside the tall windows the harbor sparkled in the October sunshine of 1870.

Twenty other men filled the room, most of them older than his thirty-five years, all of them hoping to join the ranks of certificated masters who could command deep-water vessels under the British flag. Some had been trying for years—Elias recognized Peterson from the *Mariner's Rest*, a competent first mate who had failed the examination twice already. Others, like himself, were taking it for the first time, their confidence built on years of steady advancement through the ranks.

The written portion had gone well enough. Questions on navigation, seamanship, maritime law, and cargo handling —subjects he had been studying for two years while serving as chief mate aboard various vessels. But the real test would come this afternoon, when Captain Sir William Morrison—no relation to his current drunkard captain— would conduct the oral examination that separated the truly competent from the merely ambitious.

"Mr. Johnson?" The clerk's voice cut through his concentration. "Captain Morrison will see you now."

The examination room was austere, dominated by a large chart table and shelves lined with the tools of navigation—sextants, chronometers, parallel rulers, and well-worn volumes of sailing directions. Captain Morrison himself was a slight man with piercing blue eyes and the kind of weathered face that spoke of forty years before the mast. He had commanded some of the finest ships in the North Atlantic trade, and his reputation for fairness was matched only by his intolerance for incompetence.

"Sit down, Mr. Johnson." Morrison's voice carried the authority of long command. "I've reviewed your written examination. Creditable work, though I note you favor the lunar distance method for determining longitude when a chronometer is unavailable."

"Yes, sir. In my experience, it's more reliable than dead reckoning over long passages, particularly in the North Atlantic where weather can prevent sight-taking for days at a time."

Morrison nodded approvingly. "Practical experience speaking, I see. Now then, let's say you're bound from Saint John to Liverpool with a cargo of timber. Three days out, you encounter a gale from the northwest. Your fore topsail splits along the bolt rope, you're taking green water over the bows, and your second mate reports the deck cargo is working loose. What are your orders?"

For the next hour, Morrison presented scenario after scenario, each one designed to test not just technical knowledge but judgment under pressure. A fire in the cargo hold while anchored in a foreign port with no assistance available. A crew mutiny in mid-ocean with the officers divided in their loyalties. A collision with another vessel in fog, with both ships damaged and blame uncertain.

Elias answered each question carefully, drawing on his years of experience while being mindful that Morrison was evaluating not just his knowledge but his character. A ship's master was responsible for more than navigation and seamanship—he was judge, diplomat, father figure, and final authority in a world where the nearest help might be a thousand miles away.

"One final question, Mr. Johnson." Morrison leaned back in his chair, his eyes studying Elias with careful attention. "I've heard some interesting reports from the crew of the *Cassandra* about your recent voyage—something about going aloft in a blow to secure a torn topsail while your captain was... indisposed. Some might say that's admirable seamanship. Others might call it showing off, or exceeding your authority as First Mate. What's your view on when an officer should lead by example, and when such actions might undermine proper chain of command?"

It was, Elias realized, both a test of his judgment and a probe into his character. Morrison had clearly spoken to members of the *Cassandra's* crew—perhaps at the

Mariner's Rest or one of Halifax's other sailor haunts. The examiner wanted to know whether Elias was a glory-seeker who put personal heroics above proper procedure, or an officer who understood when duty required going beyond the normal bounds of rank.

"The ship needed that sail secured, sir," Elias said carefully. "In those conditions, sending a less experienced man aloft would have been dangerous—possibly fatal. I had the skill to do the job safely, and as First Mate, I was responsible for the ship's welfare when the captain was unable to perform his duties." He paused, considering his next words. "But you're right to ask about chain of command. I made sure the crew understood that what they saw was necessity, not routine. An officer who makes a habit of doing the crew's work isn't leading—he's just showing that he doesn't trust his subordinates to do their jobs."

Morrison was quiet for a long moment, making notes on a sheet of paper. When he looked up, there was something that might have been approval in his eyes.

"Very well, Mr. Johnson. You'll receive official notification within the week, but I can tell you now that you've passed. You have your master's certificate." He stood and extended his hand. "I hope you'll use it wisely."

Three weeks later, Elias stood on the quarterdeck of the barque *Providence*, watching the stevedores load the last of their cargo while Yarmouth harbor bustled around them with its usual purposeful chaos. His own ship. His own command. The knowledge still felt unreal, like something that might evaporate if he examined it too closely.

The *Providence* was no beauty—a workmanlike vessel of four hundred tons, built for carrying cargo rather than impressing passengers. But she was sound, well-found, and now she was his responsibility. More importantly, the owners had given him the freedom to choose his own officers, a privilege that many new masters didn't enjoy.

"Mr. Brennan reporting for duty, sir."

Elias turned to find Thomas Brennan standing at the head of the gangway, sea bag over his shoulder and an expression of barely concealed expectation on his face. They had sailed together twice in the past three years, and Brennan had been dropping increasingly obvious hints about his hopes for advancement when Elias achieved command.

"Mr. Brennan. Welcome aboard." Elias kept his voice neutral, professional. "I trust you had a pleasant journey from Halifax?"

"Pleasant enough, sir. I confess I'm eager to learn what position you have in mind for me." Brennan's smile held an edge of presumption that set Elias's teeth on edge. "I know you value experienced officers."

It was a delicate moment, the kind that could shape relationships for an entire voyage. Brennan was competent, certainly—he knew his business and could handle a watch as well as most. But there was something in his manner, a calculating ambition that made Elias uneasy. Leadership required more than technical skill; it required the ability to put the ship's welfare above personal advancement.

"I do indeed value experience," Elias said carefully. "But I also value judgment and reliability. I'll be making my officer assignments this evening, once I've spoken with all the candidates."

The flash of anger in Brennan's eyes was quickly suppressed, but not quickly enough. "Of course, sir. I'm sure you'll make the right choice."

After Brennan disappeared below to stow his gear, Elias returned to his contemplation of the harbor. The conversation had confirmed his instincts about the man—capable but ambitious, the kind of officer who would question orders if he disagreed with them, who would put his own advancement above the ship's welfare if the situation presented itself.

"Captain Johnson?"

He turned to find a young man standing respectfully at attention, cap in hand. Fair-haired and slight of build, with the kind of earnest expression that marked him as either very green or very dedicated.

"I'm Robert Hartwell, sir. I believe you're expecting me?"

Indeed he was. Hartwell had been recommended by Captain Williams of the *Atlantic Trader*, who had described him as "the finest third mate I've sailed with in twenty years." High praise from a man not given to hyperbole.

"Mr. Hartwell. Captain Williams speaks very highly of you. I understand you've been serving as third mate for the past two years?"

"Yes, sir. On the Liverpool run, mostly. Some Caribbean voyages as well." Hartwell's voice was steady, confident without being presumptuous. "I've been hoping for advancement to second mate, sir. I know I'm young, but I believe I'm ready for the responsibility."

Elias studied the young officer's face, noting the directness of his gaze, the way he stood without fidgeting despite the obvious importance of this moment to his career. There was something about Hartwell that reminded him of his own younger self—the eagerness to prove himself, tempered by a genuine respect for the sea and the traditions of seamanship.

"Tell me about the worst weather you've encountered, Mr. Hartwell."

"Hurricane off Cape Hatteras last year, sir. We were bound from Savannah to Boston when it caught us. Winds like nothing I'd ever seen, seas running mountain-high. We rode it out under bare poles for thirty-six hours, with the ship laying over so far I thought she'd never come back up."

"What was your role during the storm?"

"I was on deck the whole time, sir, helping to secure loose gear and keep the pumps going. The second mate was injured early on—took a fall when the ship pitched—so I found myself doing his work as well as my own."

"And the crew? How did they respond to taking orders from a third mate barely out of his teens?"

Hartwell smiled slightly. "At first they weren't too keen, sir. But when they saw I knew what I was doing, they came around. Old Murphy—he was bosun—he told me later that it wasn't about age, it was about competence. 'The sea don't care how old you are, lad,' he said. 'She only cares if you can do your job.'"

It was exactly the right answer, delivered with the kind of unconscious wisdom that couldn't be taught. Elias made his decision in that moment, though he was careful not to let it show on his face.

"Very well, Mr. Hartwell. I'll speak with you again this evening."

The rest of the afternoon was spent interviewing the other candidates—experienced men mostly, solid officers who would serve competently in whatever position they were given. But as the sun began to set over Yarmouth harbor, Elias found his thoughts returning to the contrast between

32

Brennan's presumptuous confidence and Hartwell's earnest professionalism.

He called them all together as the ship's bell struck eight o'clock, the officers gathering in the chart room while the crew went about their evening duties. Brennan stood slightly apart from the others, his expectant smile suggesting he had no doubt about the outcome.

"Gentlemen," Elias began, "I've made my decisions regarding officer assignments for this voyage. Mr. Hartwell, you'll serve as second mate."

The silence that followed was profound. Hartwell's face showed a mixture of surprise and gratification, while the other candidates accepted the news with the stoic resignation of men accustomed to disappointment. But it was Brennan's reaction that concerned Elias most—the flash of fury that transformed his features before he managed to regain control.

"Mr. Brennan, you'll continue as third mate. Mr. Peterson, I'm appointing you bosun, given your experience with cargo handling."

The formal announcement continued, but Elias could see that Brennan had stopped listening. The man's face had settled into a mask of professional composure, but his eyes held a cold anger that spoke of resentment deeply felt and likely long remembered.

After the others had dispersed to their duties, Brennan lingered, ostensibly to discuss watch arrangements but actually, Elias suspected, to register his displeasure.

"An interesting choice, sir," Brennan said, his voice carefully neutral. "Young Hartwell certainly seems... enthusiastic."

"He's competent and reliable," Elias replied evenly. "Those are the qualities I value most in an officer."

"Of course, sir. Though I confess I'm surprised you didn't consider experience more heavily in your decision. I've been at sea longer than Mr. Hartwell has been alive."

There it was—the challenge barely veiled as a question. Elias chose his words carefully, aware that this conversation would likely define their relationship for the entire voyage.

"Experience is valuable, Mr. Brennan, but it's not the only consideration. I need officers who understand that the ship comes first, always. Personal ambition, while natural, must never interfere with duty."

Brennan's smile was sharp as a blade. "I quite agree, sir. Duty before self. I'm sure we'll all remember that in the weeks to come."

After Brennan left, Elias remained in the chart room, studying the charts for their planned route to Brazil. But his mind kept returning to the conversation, to the veiled threat in Brennan's final words. He had made an enemy today, that much was clear. The question was whether his choice had been wise or foolish.

A knock at the door interrupted his thoughts. "Come."

Hartwell entered, his face showing the strain of the day's events. "Beg pardon, Captain, but I wanted to thank you for the appointment. I know it wasn't the popular choice."

"Popularity isn't my concern, Mr. Hartwell. Competence is. You've earned this position through merit, and I trust you'll continue to justify my confidence in you."

"I'll do my best, sir." Hartwell paused, then added quietly, "I should warn you—Mr. Brennan isn't pleased. He's been talking to some of the crew, suggesting that youth and inexperience might prove... problematic in difficult situations."

Elias nodded grimly. It was beginning already—the subtle undermining, the poisonous whispers designed to erode confidence in his judgment. He had seen it before on other ships, had watched good officers destroyed by campaigns of gossip and innuendo.

"Mr. Hartwell, let me give you some advice. The best response to criticism is competence. Do your job well, treat the crew fairly, and let your actions speak for themselves. As for Mr. Brennan..." Elias paused, choosing his words carefully. "He's an experienced officer who feels passed over. That's understandable. But if he puts his personal grievances above the ship's welfare, that's a different matter entirely."

After Hartwell left, Elias walked out onto the deck, breathing in the familiar scents of salt air and tar. Around him, the *Providence* settled into the rhythms of evening—the watch change, the careful checking of lines and rigging, the quiet conversations of men preparing for another night at anchor.

Tomorrow they would sail, carrying their cargo of timber and their crew of twenty-three souls toward the distant shores of Brazil. It would be his first voyage as master, his first real test of the judgment and leadership that had earned him command. The knowledge was both exhilarating and sobering.

He thought of his mother, probably sitting by her window at this very moment, watching the lights of the anchored ships and thinking of her son. She would understand his choice regarding the officers—she had always valued character over convenience, had taught him that doing right was more important than being popular.

"The sea will test you," she had said when he told her about his appointment. "But more than that, command will test you. You'll have to make decisions that affect other men's lives, and some of those decisions won't be popular. The question isn't whether you'll make mistakes—you will. The question is whether you'll make them for the right reasons."

Standing on his own quarterdeck, with his first command spread around him like a kingdom of wood and canvas, Elias understood what she meant. He had made his choice regarding Brennan and Hartwell based on his judgment of their character, not their seniority or their expectations. Time would tell whether that judgment was sound.

But as he looked up at the stars beginning to appear in the darkening sky, he felt a quiet confidence settle over him like a familiar coat. He was ready for this—ready for the responsibility, ready for the challenges, ready to prove himself worthy of the trust that had been placed in him.

The *Providence* rocked gently at her anchor, eager for the morning tide that would carry her to sea. And on her quarterdeck, her captain stood watch, thinking of the voyage ahead and the long journey that had brought him to this moment of command.

Chapter 4: First Command

The morning of departure dawned gray and still, with fog hanging thick over Yarmouth harbor like a woolen blanket. From the *Providence's* quarterdeck, Elias could barely make out the ghostly shapes of other vessels at anchor, their masts disappearing into the murk above the crosstrees. It was the kind of weather that separated competent sailors from merely adequate ones—conditions that demanded patience, skill, and absolute confidence in one's seamanship.

But there was no wind. The harbor lay flat as a millpond, the surface broken only by the gentle swells that rolled in from the open ocean. For a sailing vessel, it presented a challenge that required both patience and ingenuity.

"All hands, prepare to warp the ship!"

His voice carried clearly through the fog, and he watched with satisfaction as the crew sprang into motion. Warping —using the ship's boats to carry anchors ahead and then hauling the vessel forward by her capstan—was back-breaking work that tested both seamanship and endurance. But it was the only way to move a sailing ship when nature provided no wind.

The crew were a mixed lot—some faces he recognized from previous voyages, others new to him but bearing the unmistakable marks of deep-water sailors. There was old Santos, a Portuguese rigger who could splice wire in a gale; Murphy, an Irishman whose knowledge of Caribbean waters was legendary; and young Collins, barely seventeen but already showing the makings of a first-rate seaman.

What mattered most was how they responded to his orders. A new captain was always an unknown quantity, regardless of his reputation or previous experience. These men would judge him not on what others said about his competence, but on what they observed with their own eyes in the days and weeks to come.

"Away the launch!" Hartwell's voice rang clear as he supervised the lowering of the ship's largest boat. Six men tumbled into it, along with a kedge anchor and several hundred fathoms of heavy line. It would be slow work— drop the kedge ahead of the ship, make fast the line to the capstan, heave the ship forward, then repeat the process until they reached deeper water where the tide might give them steerage way.

Elias positioned himself where he could oversee the operation while keeping watch for other vessels in the fog. Yarmouth harbor was always busy, and collision was a constant danger when visibility was limited to a few dozen yards in any direction.

"Handsomely there!" he called as the launch disappeared into the gray murk. "Mind the shoal water off Devil's Half Acre!"

The reply came faintly through the fog—Hartwell acknowledging the warning from his position in the boat's stern sheets. The young second mate was proving himself competent at boat handling as well as deck work, another good sign for the voyage ahead.

The first warp took nearly an hour. Elias listened to the rhythmic clank of the capstan pawls as the crew walked it around, hauling the *Providence* slowly through the still water. It was exhausting work, but necessary—and it gave him a chance to observe his men under stress.

They worked well together, he noted with satisfaction. Santos directed the foredeck operations with the quiet authority of long experience, while Murphy kept the capstan crew working in rhythm with a string of nautical songs that would have made a preacher blush. Most importantly, they responded promptly to orders from both himself and his officers.

"Kedge's up, sir!" The call came from the launch as it emerged from the fog like a ghost ship. "Ready for the next warp!"

Two more warps brought them to the harbor mouth, where a slight breeze finally began to stir the fog. Elias felt it on his cheek—barely more than a whisper from the northeast, but enough to give them steerage way once they set canvas.

"Hoist the launch. All hands make sail!"

The transition from warping to sailing was always a relief, like throwing off shackles and letting the ship find her natural element. Canvas blossomed along the *Providence's* yards—foresail, fore topsail, main topsail, jib. Not enough wind yet for the lighter sails, but sufficient to give them way through the water.

As they cleared the harbor mouth, the fog began to thin, revealing patches of blue sky and the distant outline of the Nova Scotia coast. The wind was still light but steadying from the northeast—fair for their southward course toward the Brazilian ports.

"She answers the helm well, sir." Collins, who had been assigned to the wheel, spoke with the easy confidence of a natural helmsman. "Bit of weather helm, but nothing to trouble about."

Elias nodded approvingly. A good helmsman could feel a ship's character through the spokes of the wheel, could sense her moods and preferences as clearly as a rider knew his horse. Collins had that gift, rare in one so young.

"Two points to starboard. We'll stand well clear of Seal Island before shaping our course for the Gulf Stream."

The morning passed quietly as they worked their way offshore, the wind gradually strengthening and the fog lifting to reveal a gray but navigable sea. Elias found himself settling into the familiar rhythms of command— checking their position, watching the weather signs, observing his crew and officers as they went about their duties.

It was during the noon watch that Brennan approached him, ostensibly to report on the ship's progress but actually, Elias suspected, to probe for weaknesses he might exploit.

"Making good time now, sir," the third mate said, his pale eyes fixed on the crew working in the rigging. "The men seem to be settling in well enough. Though some of them were asking about your experience as master. Natural curiosity, I suppose, given that this is your first command."

There it was   subtle but unmistakable. Brennan was spreading doubt about his captain's qualifications, playing on the natural nervousness that came with sailing under an untested master. It was exactly the kind of behavior Elias had expected, and exactly the reason he had chosen Hartwell over the more senior officer.

"I'm sure they were," Elias said mildly, not taking his eyes from the compass. "And what did you tell them?"

Brennan's smile was sharp as winter ice. "Why, that you've served as first mate on several fine vessels, and that Captain Morrison himself signed your master's certificate. What else would I tell them?"

The words were perfectly correct, but the tone suggested that these qualifications might not be sufficient for the challenges ahead. It was a masterful piece of insubordination—technically respectful but practically corrosive.

"Indeed," Elias replied evenly. "Though I suspect the crew will form their own opinions based on what they observe, rather than what they're told. Sailors are practical men, Mr. Brennan. They tend to judge officers by results rather than rumors."

The barb hit home—Elias could see it in the momentary tightening around Brennan's eyes. But the man recovered quickly, his expression returning to its mask of professional neutrality.

"Of course, sir. Results are what matter at sea." Brennan paused, then added with studied casualness, "I trust you won't hesitate to call on my experience if circumstances require it. Twenty years before the mast teaches a man a few tricks that might prove useful."

It was both an offer and a threat—Brennan positioning himself as the voice of experience while subtly suggesting that youth and inexperience might prove inadequate when the sea showed its teeth. Elias filed the conversation away for future reference while maintaining his outward calm.

"I value the experience of all my officers, Mr. Brennan. But I trust you understand that final responsibility rests with the master, regardless of his age or the length of his service."

After Brennan moved away to attend to his duties, Elias remained at the rail, watching the Nova Scotia coast fade into the afternoon haze. The confrontation had been subtle but significant—Brennan had declared his intentions without quite crossing the line into open insubordination. It was the beginning of what would likely be a long campaign of whispered doubts and veiled challenges.

But Elias had faced ambitious subordinates before, had seen how they operated and how they could be countered. The key was to maintain discipline without appearing insecure, to demonstrate competence without seeming to show off. Most importantly, he needed to earn the crew's confidence through his actions rather than his words.

"Mr. Hartwell," he called as the young second mate passed within earshot. "Take a bearing on Seal Island Light, if you please. I want our position precisely plotted before we lose sight of the land."

It was a routine order, the kind any prudent navigator would give. But Elias was also making a point—that he intended to navigate by careful observation and calculation rather than guesswork or luck. The crew would notice such things, would file them away as evidence of their captain's competence or lack thereof.

As the afternoon wore on and the *Providence* settled into her stride, Elias found himself cautiously optimistic about the voyage ahead. The ship handled well, responding to sail changes with the alacrity of a well-bred horse. The crew worked efficiently, showing the kind of professional skill that made complex evolutions look effortless. Even

Brennan, despite his obvious resentment, was performing his duties competently.

But it was still early days. The real tests would come when they encountered their first serious weather, when decisions had to be made quickly and accurately in conditions where mistakes could prove fatal. That was when reputations were made or broken, when the theoretical knowledge gained from books and examinations met the practical realities of wind and wave.

The sun was setting behind them, painting the western sky in shades of orange and gold, when Collins reported the first real breeze of the voyage.

"Wind's freshening from the nor'east, sir. Steady force four, maybe five."

Elias nodded with satisfaction. Perfect sailing weather for their course south. "Very good. Set the main topgallant and fore topgallant. We'll make the most of this breeze while it lasts."

The order was passed forward, and within minutes the *Providence* was carrying additional canvas, her speed increasing noticeably as she responded to the fuller press of sail. Elias felt the familiar thrill that came with a ship running free—the sense of partnership between human skill and natural force that made sailing more art than science.

By full dark, they were well clear of the coast, heading south-southeast toward the Gulf Stream and the open

Atlantic beyond. The wind held steady, the seas were moderate, and the ship was making good time on her course. It had been, Elias reflected, about as good a first day as any captain could hope for.

But as he prepared to go below for his evening meal, he caught sight of Brennan talking quietly with several of the crew near the galley. The conversation stopped abruptly when the men noticed their captain's attention, but not before Elias had seen the calculating look in Brennan's eyes.

The campaign of whispers had begun in earnest. The question now was whether Elias could establish his authority firmly enough to counter it before it poisoned the entire crew's confidence in his leadership.

Time would tell. But as he descended to his cabin, Elias felt the quiet confidence that had carried him through twenty-three years at sea. He had handled ambitious subordinates before, had weathered storms both meteorological and political. This voyage would test him in new ways, but he was ready for whatever challenges lay ahead.

The *Providence* sailed on through the night, carrying her crew toward the distant shores of Brazil and whatever adventures awaited them there.

Chapter 5: Trial by Storm

Four days out from Yarmouth, Elias began reading the signs that spelled trouble ahead.

It started with the barometer—a steady, persistent drop that spoke of something large and violent moving up from the Caribbean. But there were other indicators that his twenty-three years at sea had taught him to recognize: the peculiar quality of the morning light, the way the swells had begun running from multiple directions, the nervous behavior of the seabirds that had been following the ship since they entered the Gulf Stream.

"Glass has dropped six points since yesterday morning, sir." Hartwell's voice carried concern as he reported the noon observations. "And those clouds to the southwest—they've got an ugly look about them."

Elias nodded, his weathered face grim with professional assessment. He had been watching those distant clouds for hours, noting how they built and dissipated in patterns that suggested tremendous forces at work beyond the horizon. The wind, which had been fair and steady from the northeast, was beginning to back toward the east—never a good sign in these waters during hurricane season.

"We're in for a proper blow," Elias said quietly, his eyes still fixed on the southwestern horizon. "Hurricane, by the look of those signs. Born somewhere down in the Caribbean and tracking north along the coast." He turned to face his second mate. "Pass the word for all hands, Mr. Hartwell. We'll strip her down to storm canvas now, while we have time to do it properly."

The order might have seemed premature to a landsman— the immediate weather was still moderate, with nothing to suggest the violence that lay ahead. But Hartwell had sailed with experienced captains before, and he recognized the wisdom of early preparation.

"Strip to storm canvas, aye sir. And the boats?"

"Double-lashed and covered. Extra gaskets on all sails we're taking in. And Mr. Hartwell—" Elias's voice carried the weight of hard-won experience. "Make sure the men understand this isn't drill. In twelve hours, maybe less, we're going to be fighting for our lives."

The preparations took the better part of the afternoon, carried out with the methodical thoroughness that marked the difference between professional seamanship and mere sailing. Canvas came down yard by yard—topgallants first, then topsails, then courses—until the *Providence* showed only her storm trysail, storm staysail, and a small triangle of headsail to maintain steerage way.

Elias supervised every aspect of the evolution, his experienced eye catching details that could mean the difference between survival and disaster. Extra gaskets on the furled sails to prevent them tearing loose in the wind. Storm lashings on the boats that would hold even if the ship buried her rail completely. The spare anchors rigged with heavy chain, ready to deploy if the storm drove them toward dangerous shoals.

"Secure the galley fire," he ordered as the wind began to freshen. "Cold food only until this blows over. And see that the fresh water casks are double-lashed—if we lose our drinking water, the storm will be the least of our worries."

By late afternoon, with the barometer still falling and the wind backing further south, the *Providence* was as ready as human skill could make her. The crew had worked with the quiet efficiency that came from understanding exactly what they faced, and Elias felt a surge of professional pride at how smoothly the preparations had gone.

"That's proper seamanship," Santos observed as he secured the last of the deck cargo. "Many captains, they wait too long, try to carry sail until the last minute. Then when the blow comes, no time to do things right."

It was high praise from the Portuguese rigger, whose thirty years before the mast had shown him every kind of weather the Atlantic could produce. More importantly, Elias could see the crew's confidence in their preparations —and in their captain's judgment. They had time to double-check every lashing, to stow every loose article, to mentally prepare for what lay ahead.

As if summoned by Santos's words, the wind began to freshen, backing further toward the south and bringing with it the first hints of the violence to come. The sea, which had been running in long, easy swells, began to steepen and grow confused as competing wind patterns fought for dominance. The *Providence* started to pitch more heavily, her motion becoming short and uncomfortable as she encountered the storm's outer bands.

"Mr. Brennan!" Elias spotted the third mate directing the securing of the longboat. "See that the storm anchors are ready to deploy. We may need them if this blow drives us toward shallow water."

Brennan looked up from his work, his pale eyes holding a glint that might have been anticipation. "Storm anchors, sir? Surely that's a bit premature. We're still in deep water, and the weather may not prove as severe as you think."

It was a calculated challenge, delivered in front of half the crew. Brennan was questioning not just the specific order but Elias's judgment in preparing for the worst-case scenario. The men paused in their work, sensing the tension crackling between their officers like electricity before lightning.

"Mr. Brennan," Elias said quietly, his voice carrying absolute authority, "when I give an order, I expect it to be carried out immediately and without discussion. The time for debate is before we face the storm, not during it."

For a moment, the two men stared at each other across the deck, the crew watching with the fascination that comes from witnessing a confrontation between authority and ambition. Then Brennan's gaze dropped, and he nodded curtly.

"Aye, sir. Storm anchors it is."

But Elias caught the look that passed between Brennan and Murphy, the Irishman who served as bosun. A look that spoke of private conversations and shared doubts about their captain's experience. He filed it away for future reference, knowing that such moments of weakness could prove fatal if allowed to fester.

The storm struck at sunset with the sudden fury of divine wrath.

One moment the *Providence* was running under shortened sail through increasingly heavy seas, the next she was buried rail-deep in green water as hurricane-force winds swept across her decks like the breath of some primordial monster. The barometer, which had been falling steadily all day, suddenly plummeted as if weighted with lead.

"All hands on deck!" Elias roared, though his voice was nearly lost in the howling wind. "Secure for hurricane!"

The crew responded with the desperate efficiency of men who knew their survival depended on speed and coordination. But even as they worked, the storm was growing stronger, the wind rising from gale force to something that defied measurement—a shrieking demon that seemed determined to tear the very masts from the ship.

The *Providence* heeled far over to starboard as a particularly vicious gust struck her remaining canvas, and Elias felt her shudder as she fought to right herself. Water cascaded over the weather rail in solid sheets, turning the deck into a treacherous skating rink where a single misstep could mean death.

"Storm trysail's tearing itself to pieces!" Hartwell appeared at his elbow, shouting to make himself heard above the wind. "Should we try to take it in?"

Elias looked up at the small triangular sail, noting how it flogged and cracked with each gust. Without it, they would have no way to keep the ship's head up to the wind —she would broach and roll over, taking all hands with her. But if the sail tore completely away, the result would be the same.

"Take four good men and get it clewed up!" he shouted back. "But don't try to furl it—just get it gathered in! We'll ride this out under bare poles!"

It was a desperate gamble. Running before a hurricane under no sail at all meant trusting entirely to the ship's natural stability and the helmsman's skill. But it was their only choice if they wanted to survive the next few hours.

Hartwell nodded and disappeared into the chaos, gathering Santos, Collins, and two other experienced hands. Elias watched them make their way forward, timing their movements to the ship's violent pitching, each man responsible not just for his own safety but for the lives of everyone aboard.

"She's taking water fast!" Murphy appeared from below, his face grim with more than just spray. "The pump's barely keeping up, and that timber cargo is starting to shift!"

Shifting cargo was every captain's nightmare—thousands of tons of lumber breaking free from its lashings and smashing from side to side with each roll of the ship. If they couldn't control it, the *Providence* would quickly become top-heavy and unstable, ready to capsize at the first opportunity.

"Get every available man on the pumps," Elias ordered. "And see if you can re-secure that cargo. Use anything you can find—spare line, chain, even the anchor cable if you have to."

Murphy nodded grimly and disappeared below, taking half a dozen men with him. That left barely enough hands on deck to manage the ship, but there was no choice. If they couldn't control the water and cargo below, nothing they did topside would matter.

The storm raged through the night with undiminished fury. Waves the size of mountains rolled out of the darkness, their crests torn away by the wind and hurled horizontally across the sea like grapeshot. The *Providence* climbed each one with agonizing slowness, hung for a terrifying moment on the crest, then plunged into the trough beyond with a bone-jarring crash that seemed to shake every timber in her hull.

Elias remained at his post throughout the ordeal, moving between the wheel and the weather rail, watching for the rogue wave or wind shift that could destroy them in an instant. His oilskins were torn and streaming, his hands raw from gripping lifelines, but he stayed where his crew could see him—a fixed point of authority in a world gone mad.

It was during the darkest hour before dawn that the real crisis came.

"Captain!" Collins appeared from nowhere, his face white with terror. "The foremast! She's working loose at the partners!"

Elias looked forward and felt his heart sink. The *Providence's* foremast, weakened by the constant strain of the storm, was moving in its housing with each roll of the ship. If it went by the board, the falling spars and rigging would likely take the mainmast with it, leaving them helpless in the hurricane's grip.

"Get axes!" he shouted. "If she starts to go, we'll cut her away before she takes the whole rig with her!"

But even as he gave the order, Elias knew they faced an impossible choice. Cutting away the foremast would leave them virtually helpless, unable to make sail even when the storm passed. But if they tried to save it and failed, they would lose everything.

Santos appeared with an armload of axes, his eyes meeting Elias's with perfect understanding. The old rigger had seen this situation before, knew the terrible calculus that faced any captain in such circumstances.

"What are your orders, Cap'n?"

It was the moment every master dreaded—when seamanship and experience mattered less than raw courage and the willingness to make decisions that could save or damn everyone under his command. Elias felt the weight of twenty-three lives pressing down on him like a physical force.

"We try to save her," he said finally. "Get lines around the mast heel and set up a Spanish windlass. If we can take the strain off the partners, she might hold together."

It was desperate work in appalling conditions. Men crawled across the flooded deck, passing heavy lines around the base of the mast while the ship pitched and rolled like a thing possessed. Twice, sailors were nearly washed overboard, saved only by their lifelines and the quick reflexes of their mates.

But somehow, incredibly, they managed it. The Spanish windlass—a simple arrangement of ropes and spars that could exert tremendous force—gradually took the strain off the damaged mast step. The dangerous working motion slowed, then stopped entirely.

The foremast held.

By noon the next day, the hurricane had blown itself out, leaving the *Providence* alone on a sullen gray sea that still heaved with the memory of violence. The ship was battered but intact, her crew exhausted but triumphant. They had faced the worst the Atlantic could throw at them and emerged victorious.

Elias stood at the taffrail, surveying the damage with the practiced eye of a professional seaman. Torn sails, damaged rigging, and a foremast that would need careful nursing until they could effect proper repairs. But nothing that couldn't be fixed with time, skill, and the kind of seamanship that turned disasters into mere inconveniences.

"Damage report, Mr. Hartwell."

The young second mate approached with a slate covered in careful notations. "Two sails blown away completely—the main topgallant and fore staysail. The foremast's damaged but secure. We took on about four feet of water in the hold, but the pumps have her dry now. And the cargo..." He paused, consulting his notes. "We lost about ten percent of the deck load, but the hold cargo's secure."

All things considered, it could have been much worse. Ships had been lost entirely to storms less severe than the one they had just weathered. The fact that the *Providence* was still afloat and seaworthy was testament to her construction, her crew's skill, and—Elias hoped—his own competent handling of the crisis.

"Very good, Mr. Hartwell. Set the crew to making repairs. I want new sails bent on and the rigging surveyed before we make any significant canvas."

As Hartwell moved away to relay the orders, Elias became aware of a presence at his shoulder. He turned to find Murphy, the Irish bosun, standing with his cap in his hands.

"Beggin' your pardon, Captain, but I wanted to say something about last night."

Elias nodded, curious about what the experienced sailor might have observed during the storm.

"I've sailed with a lot of masters in my time," Murphy continued, his voice rough with emotion. "Some good, some bad, some that were just lucky enough not to kill us all. But what you did last night—keepin' your head when the rest of us were half-mad with fear, makin' the right decisions when everything was goin' to hell..." He paused, searching for words. "That was real seamanship, sir. The lads know it, and they're talkin' about it."

The praise meant more than Murphy probably realized. Elias had spent the storm wondering if he was making the right choices, if his inexperience as a master might prove fatal to his crew. To hear that his decisions had been sound, that his leadership had been effective, lifted a weight from his shoulders that he hadn't even realized he was carrying.

"Thank you, Murphy. But it wasn't just my doing. The crew performed magnificently—every man did his duty when it mattered most."

"Aye, sir, that's true enough. But a crew's only as good as the man who leads them. And after last night..." Murphy straightened his shoulders, his weathered face showing something that might have been pride. "Well, sir, there's not a man aboard who wouldn't follow you into hell itself if you asked it of them."

After Murphy left to supervise the repairs, Elias remained at the rail, watching the crew work with new eyes. The storm had indeed changed something fundamental in their relationship. Where before he had been an unknown quantity, a captain to be evaluated and judged, he was now their proven leader—a man who had guided them through mortal danger and brought them out alive.

Even Brennan seemed affected by the transformation. The third mate went about his duties with less obvious resentment, his challenges to Elias's authority notably absent. Perhaps the storm had shown him something about the true nature of command—that it required more than ambition or seniority to lead men effectively in crisis.

Or perhaps he was simply biding his time, waiting for the next opportunity to undermine his captain's authority. With men like Brennan, one never knew for certain.

But for now, it was enough that the *Providence* was safe, her crew was intact, and their destination still lay ahead of them. The hurricane had been a test, and they had passed it with colors flying. Whatever challenges awaited them in Brazilian waters, Elias felt confident they could be met and overcome.

The ship settled into her new heading, her patched sails drawing well in the moderate breeze that had followed the storm. Rio de Janeiro lay still a thousand miles to the south, but for the first time since leaving Yarmouth, Elias felt truly confident in his command.

He had faced the sea's fury and emerged victorious. Now he was ready for whatever else the voyage might bring.

Chapter 6: London Bound

The harbor of Rio de Janeiro spread before them like a jewel set in emerald hills, its waters sparkling under the Southern Hemisphere sun as the *Providence* worked her way toward the anchorage. Three weeks had passed since the hurricane, three weeks of steady sailing through the trade winds while the crew repaired storm damage and settled into the comfortable rhythms of a well-run ship.

Elias stood at the quarterdeck rail, watching the busy harbor traffic with the satisfaction of a man who had brought his first command safely to its destination. The voyage had been everything he could have hoped for—profitable cargo delivered intact, crew performing like veterans, and his own reputation as master firmly established. Even Brennan had seemed to accept his authority, though Elias remained watchful for signs of renewed resentment.

"Magnificent sight, isn't it, sir?" Hartwell appeared beside him, his young face bright with the wonder that came from seeing Rio's dramatic setting for the first time. "Like something from a storybook."

"Aye, it's a fine harbor," Elias agreed, though his attention was focused more on practical matters than scenic beauty. "Good holding ground, well-protected from the weather, and deep water right up to the wharves. That's what makes it valuable to sailors, not just the view."

It was the kind of observation that marked the difference between a tourist and a professional seaman. Elias had learned long ago to appreciate natural beauty, but never to let it distract from the business of seamanship. Harbors were judged by their utility, not their appearance.

The anchorage was crowded with vessels from every corner of the globe—American whalers fresh from the Pacific grounds, British mail steamers on their regular runs, German merchantmen carrying manufactured goods to South America's growing markets. But what caught Elias's attention was the cluster of Nova Scotian vessels near the inner harbor, their familiar lines and rigging marking them as products of Maritime shipyards.

"There's the *Acadia*," he observed, pointing to a familiar barque lying at anchor near the commercial wharf. "Captain Henderson's command. Good man—sailed with him years ago when I was second mate."

The sight of other Nova Scotian vessels gave him a warm feeling of connection to home. The Maritime shipping community was small and tight-knit, bound together by shared experiences and mutual dependence. Success in these waters depended as much on reputation and trust as on seamanship and luck.

Within hours of anchoring, the *Providence* was surrounded by the usual harbor traffic—customs officials, cargo brokers, ship chandlers, and the inevitable collection of hopeful merchants looking to sell everything from fresh fruit to dubious nautical supplies. Elias received them all with professional courtesy, but his real attention was focused on the cargo brokers who would determine the success of this voyage.

"Captain Johnson?" A well-dressed Brazilian approached the gangway, his English accented but clear. "I am Senhor Oliveira, representing the coffee exporters' association. I understand you have space available for return cargo?"

Indeed he did. The timber had been discharged with remarkable efficiency, leaving the *Providence's* holds empty and ready for whatever cargo would pay the best rates for the homeward passage. Coffee was always in demand in Nova Scotia, but so were sugar, hides, and the precious hardwoods that commanded premium prices in North American furniture shops.

The negotiations took the better part of two days, conducted with the elaborate courtesy that marked South American business dealings. But when they concluded, Elias felt a surge of satisfaction. The cargo they would carry home—premium coffee beans, raw sugar, and a small consignment of rosewood—would generate profits that would impress even the most demanding shipowners.

It was while supervising the loading of this cargo that he received unexpected news.

"Captain Johnson?" The speaker was a young man in the blue uniform of the Royal Mail Steam Packet Company, his brass buttons gleaming in the tropical sun. "I have a message for you from Halifax."

The envelope bore the seal of Morrison & Company, the shipping firm that owned the *Providence*. Elias opened it with some curiosity, wondering what news could be important enough to send by fast steamer rather than waiting for his return.

The contents made him whistle softly under his breath.

Captain Johnson, the letter began in the firm handwriting of old Samuel Morrison himself. *Your handling of the September hurricane, as reported by your crew upon arrival in Rio, has impressed us considerably. We are therefore pleased to offer you command of our newest vessel, the barque* Intrepid, *presently under construction at the Morrison yards. This vessel will be assigned to the London trade, our most prestigious route, with cargo and passenger accommodations. Your appointment will commence upon completion of your current voyage.*

The London trade. It was the pinnacle of North Atlantic commerce, the route that separated first-class captains from merely competent ones. Ships on the London run carried the finest cargoes, the most important passengers, and commanded the highest rates. More importantly, they attracted the attention of the major shipping companies that controlled the most lucrative contracts.

"Good news, sir?" Hartwell had approached quietly, noting his captain's expression.

"Very good news, Mr. Hartwell. It seems our voyage has been more successful than we realized." Elias folded the letter carefully, his mind already racing ahead to the implications. "Tell me—how would you feel about a permanent position as second mate? On a larger vessel, better pay, more responsibility?"

The young officer's face lit up with undisguised pleasure. "I'd be honored, sir. Truly honored."

It was a moment of quiet triumph, the kind that made all the years of hard work and careful advancement worthwhile. Elias had brought his first command safely to port, had proven himself under the most challenging conditions, and now found himself offered one of the most coveted positions in the Maritime shipping trade.

But even as he savored the moment, he was aware of Brennan watching from across the deck, the third mate's pale eyes holding their familiar expression of calculation and resentment. The man had said nothing about his own future prospects, had made no requests for advancement or increased responsibility. But Elias could practically feel the jealousy radiating from him like heat from a stove.

The loading continued for another week, with the *Providence's* holds gradually filling with the aromatic treasure of Brazilian commerce. Coffee beans from the high plantations, their rich scent mingling with the tar and hemp of the ship's rigging. Raw sugar in heavy sacks, destined for the refineries of Halifax and Saint John. And in the most secure part of the hold, carefully padded and protected, the rosewood that would become fine furniture in the workshops of Nova Scotia's craftsmen.

It was while overseeing the final stages of cargo handling that Elias encountered Captain Henderson of the *Acadia*, the man he had pointed out to Hartwell upon their arrival.

"Johnson!" Henderson's weathered face creased in a genuine smile as he approached the *Providence's* gangway. "Heard you'd finally got your own command. About time, I'd say—you've been ready for it longer than most."

The two men shook hands with the easy familiarity of old shipmates, and Henderson accepted Elias's invitation to come aboard for a drink and conversation. It was one of the pleasures of foreign ports—the chance to exchange news and stories with fellow mariners, to maintain the bonds that held the shipping community together across thousands of miles of ocean.

"Fine vessel," Henderson observed as they toured the *Providence's* deck. "Morrison builds them well, always has. And I hear you've been offered the new barque they're constructing—the *Intrepid*?"

Word traveled fast in the close-knit world of Maritime shipping. Elias nodded, curious about what Henderson might know about his new appointment.

"London trade, so I'm told. That's a plum assignment for a first voyage as master. Morrison must think highly of your abilities."

"I hope to justify his confidence," Elias replied diplomatically. "Though I suspect the real test will come when we encounter North Atlantic weather in winter."

Henderson laughed, the sound carrying genuine appreciation for the challenges that lay ahead. "Spoken like a true sailor. But from what I hear about your handling of that hurricane, you've already proven you can manage a ship in heavy weather. The crew of the mail steamer that brought news from Halifax had some interesting stories to tell about Captain Johnson's seamanship."

It was gratifying to learn that his reputation was spreading beyond his own ship, that other captains were taking notice of his competence and leadership. In the Maritime shipping trade, reputation was everything—the difference between command of a first-class vessel and relegation to coastal trading or worse.

They spent the evening discussing routes, weather patterns, and the ever-changing dynamics of international commerce. Henderson, with fifteen years of experience in South American waters, was a valuable source of information about ports, agents, and the political situations that could affect shipping. But more than that, he was a link to the broader community of Nova Scotian masters who carried their province's flag to every corner of the globe.

"One word of advice about the London trade," Henderson said as the evening drew to a close. "The competition's fierce, and not always conducted on gentlemanly terms. You'll find yourself sailing against captains who've been on that route for decades, men who know every trick for gaining advantage in cargo rates and sailing schedules.

Don't let courtesy blind you to the realities of commercial warfare."

It was sage counsel, delivered with the frankness that marked true friendship. Elias filed it away for future reference, understanding that his new appointment would bring challenges beyond mere seamanship and navigation.

The *Providence* sailed from Rio on a brilliant morning in early November, her holds full and her crew in good spirits. The homeward passage promised to be routine— the hurricane season was ending, the trade winds were reliable, and they carried cargo that would command good prices in Halifax.

But for Elias, the voyage represented something more than mere commercial success. It was the completion of his first command, the proof that he could handle the responsibilities of master with competence and distinction. More importantly, it was the foundation for what promised to be a successful career in the upper ranks of the Maritime shipping trade.

As the Brazilian coast faded into the morning haze, he stood at the taffrail watching their wake stretch away toward the southern horizon. Three months ago, he had been an untested captain hoping to prove himself worthy of command. Now he was a master with a successful voyage behind him and the promise of greater opportunities ahead.

The London trade beckoned, with all its challenges and rewards. And Elias Johnson, master mariner, felt ready to meet whatever the North Atlantic might throw at him.

But even as he savored the moment of triumph, he remained aware of the undercurrents that could complicate future success. Brennan's resentment had not disappeared, merely been suppressed by the successful completion of their Brazilian voyage. And the shipping trade itself was changing, with steam beginning to challenge sail on the most profitable routes.

For now, though, such concerns seemed distant and manageable. The *Providence* was heading home with a profitable cargo, his crew was performing with professional excellence, and his own reputation as a competent master was firmly established.

The future, whatever it might bring, would have to take care of itself.

Chapter 7: Whaler's Wrath

The *Intrepid* was everything Elias had hoped she would be and more. Four hundred and fifty tons of Nova Scotia craftsmanship, built from the finest timber the Maritime forests could provide, her lines were those of a vessel designed for speed and seaworthiness in equal measure. She carried the latest innovations in rigging and sail plan, improvements that promised to shave precious days off the Atlantic crossing while maintaining the reliability that had made Nova Scotia ships legendary throughout the commercial world.

Standing on her quarterdeck as they cleared Halifax harbor on a crisp morning in March of 1871, Elias felt the deep satisfaction that came from commanding a truly fine vessel. The *Intrepid* responded to every shift of wind and adjustment of sail like a thoroughbred horse answering its rider's touch. Her crew—mostly familiar faces from the *Providence*, supplemented by a few carefully chosen additions—worked with the easy competence of men who understood they were sailing aboard something special.

"She's got a turn of speed on her," Hartwell observed, his experienced eye noting how cleanly the barque cut through the water. Now confirmed as second mate, he had thrown himself into learning every detail of the new vessel's handling characteristics.

"That she does," Elias agreed, watching the log line trail astern as they settled onto their eastbound course.

"Morrison outdid himself with this one. She'll show her heels to anything else on the London run, if we handle her right."

The London trade had proven everything Captain Henderson had warned it would be—fiercely competitive, demanding, and unforgiving of the smallest mistakes. But the *Intrepid's* speed had already given them an edge over their competitors, allowing them to maintain schedules that other vessels could only envy. Three successful passages had established their reputation among London's cargo brokers, and booking space aboard the *Intrepid* was becoming increasingly difficult as merchants competed for the fastest passage to North America.

This voyage was their most ambitious yet—a full cargo of manufactured goods, fine machinery, and textiles, plus six cabin passengers who had paid premium rates for the privilege of sailing in the newest and fastest vessel on the route. The pressure to maintain their schedule was correspondingly intense, with agents in London making promises based on the *Intrepid's* record of reliable arrivals.

It was on their fourth day out, with the Irish coast fading into the morning haze behind them, that they encountered the whalers.

Elias first spotted them from the maintop, where he had gone to take a bearing on a distant sail. Three vessels running in company, their bluff bows and try-works identifying them unmistakably as Yankee whalers bound for the Arctic grounds. They were on a converging course with the *Intrepid,* and from their spread of canvas, it was clear they meant to cross ahead of the merchant vessel.

Under normal circumstances, it would have been a routine encounter—ships passing at sea with perhaps a exchange of signals and news. But as the distance closed, Elias began to sense that something was wrong. The leading whaler was flying signals that seemed unnecessarily aggressive, and her captain was making no effort to give way despite the *Intrepid's* superior sailing qualities.

"Yankee whalers, sir," Santos called from the foredeck, his experienced eye reading the approaching vessels' intentions. "And they don't look friendly."

By noon, the situation had developed into something approaching a maritime confrontation. The lead whaler, a barque of perhaps three hundred tons, had positioned herself directly across the *Intrepid's* intended course and showed no sign of yielding the right of way. Her consorts had spread out to port and starboard, effectively blocking any attempt to pass without risking collision.

"What in blazes do they think they're doing?" Hartwell's voice carried the indignation of a professional seaman faced with inexplicable behavior. "They have no right to block a merchant vessel on the high seas."

Elias studied the whalers through his glass, noting their weather-beaten appearance and the aggressive way they were being handled. American whalers were notorious for their independence and their willingness to bend maritime law when it suited their purposes. But this behavior went beyond mere discourtesy—it bordered on piracy.

"Signal them," he ordered. "Ask their intentions."

The flag hoist brought an immediate response, but not the one Elias had expected. The lead whaler's captain appeared on his quarterdeck with a speaking trumpet, and his voice carried clearly across the water between the vessels.

"Nova Scotia vessel! You're sailing through our fishing grounds! Heave to and allow us to search for contraband!"

The demand was both outrageous and legally meaningless. There were no "fishing grounds" in international waters, and no authority that gave whalers the right to stop and search merchant vessels. But the tactical situation was undeniably serious—three vessels against one, with the whalers positioned to ram or disable the *Intrepid* if their demands were refused.

"Contraband?" Brennan's voice carried a mixture of disbelief and calculation. "What contraband could we possibly be carrying?"

It was a good question, and one that suggested this confrontation was about something more than maritime law. Elias studied the whalers' positioning again, noting how they had maneuvered to force the *Intrepid* onto a more southerly course—away from the great circle route that offered the fastest passage to Nova Scotia.

"It's not about contraband," he said quietly. "They want to delay us. Force us off our best course, cost us time and speed."

The implications were disturbing. If word of the *Intrepid's* remarkable passages had reached competitors, it was possible that rival shipping interests were paying the whalers to interfere with their schedule. Such tactics were not unknown in the cutthroat world of international commerce, though they were rarely so blatant.

"Orders, sir?" Hartwell's voice was steady, but Elias could see the tension in the young officer's shoulders. This was not a situation covered in any manual of seamanship.

Elias considered his options. He could submit to the whalers' demands, allow them to conduct their meaningless search, and accept the delay that would result. It would be the safe choice, the one that avoided immediate confrontation but effectively surrendered to maritime bullying.

Or he could refuse, assert his rights as master of a legitimate merchant vessel, and deal with whatever consequences followed.

"All hands on deck," he said finally. "We're going through them."

The order galvanized the crew into immediate action. Men sprang to the rigging, sheets and braces were overhauled, and the *Intrepid* began to show her teeth. Elias had no intention of actually ramming the whalers, but he was prepared to call their bluff and force them to choose between giving way or risking collision.

"Port your helm two points," he called to the helmsman. "We'll pass between the leader and his starboard consort."

It was a dangerous gambit, requiring precise timing and absolute confidence in his vessel's handling qualities. The gap between the whalers was narrow—perhaps two ship lengths at most—and any miscalculation could result in disaster for all concerned.

But the *Intrepid* was built for such moments. She responded to the helm like a racing yacht, gathering speed as her sails filled with the fresh westerly wind. Her reputation for speed was about to be put to the ultimate test.

"Stand by to wear ship if necessary!" Elias called, keeping his eyes fixed on the approaching gap. "But hold your course steady!"

The distance closed rapidly. Elias could see the whalers' crews lining their rails, could hear their officers shouting orders as they realized the merchant vessel was not going to submit to their demands. The lead whaler began to swing toward them, obviously intending to close the gap and force submission.

But she was too late. The *Intrepid* was already committed to her course, her speed carrying her forward with unstoppable momentum. At the last moment, with collision seeming inevitable, the whaler's nerve broke. Her captain spun his wheel hard over, swinging away from the charging merchant vessel with barely yards to spare.

The *Intrepid* shot through the gap like an arrow from a bow, her crew cheering wildly as they left the confused whalers wallowing in their wake. It had been perfectly executed—a display of seamanship and courage that would be talked about in forecastles for years to come.

But even as he accepted the crew's congratulations, Elias knew the confrontation was far from over. The whalers would not forget this humiliation, and if they encountered the *Intrepid* again—particularly in port, where the odds might be more even—there would certainly be trouble.

"That was brilliantly done, sir," Hartwell said quietly, his voice carrying genuine admiration. "I've never seen ship-handling like that."

"It was necessary," Elias replied, though he felt a surge of satisfaction at the young officer's praise. "A master who submits to bullying on the high seas won't command respect in any port."

But even as he spoke, he was calculating the cost of their dramatic escape. The encounter had forced them several miles south of their intended course, and the time spent maneuvering around the whalers had cost them precious hours. In the competitive world of the London trade, such delays could mean the difference between profit and loss.

"Mr. Hartwell, plot a new course for Halifax. Best possible speed, and factor in the time we've lost. I want to know exactly how much this little adventure has cost us."

The calculations, when completed, were sobering. The encounter with the whalers had put them nearly twelve hours behind their planned schedule—time that would be almost impossible to make up without taking risks that could endanger ship and cargo.

But as Elias watched the whalers fade into the distance astern, he felt no regret for his decision. A ship's master who allowed himself to be bullied at sea would find his authority questioned in every subsequent crisis. The *Intrepid's* reputation for speed was valuable, but her captain's reputation for firmness under pressure was even more important.

The North Atlantic stretched ahead of them, gray and endless under the March sky. Somewhere beyond the horizon lay Nova Scotia and the end of another successful voyage. But Elias knew that success would now depend not just on seamanship and favorable winds, but on their ability to overcome the delay imposed by three stubborn whalers who had chosen to test the wrong merchant captain.

The *Intrepid* sailed on through the afternoon, her crew working with renewed energy as they adjusted sail and course to make up lost time. And on her quarterdeck, her master stood watch, thinking of schedules and reputations and the sometimes harsh realities of command at sea.

The whalers had made their point. Now it remained to be seen whether Captain Elias Johnson could make his.

Chapter 8: London Trouble

The London docks sprawled along the Thames like a vast mechanical organism, alive with the constant motion of commerce and industry. Forests of masts rose from the crowded wharves, their rigging creating intricate webs against the smoky sky, while the cries of stevedores, the rumble of carts, and the whistle of steam engines created a symphony of maritime trade that never ceased, day or night.

Elias stood at the *Intrepid's* rail, watching his crew secure the ship to her assigned berth at the West India Dock. Despite the delay caused by the whaler encounter, they had made remarkably good time across the Atlantic, arriving only eighteen hours behind their published schedule. It was a testament to both the ship's speed and the crew's skill, but in the unforgiving world of commercial shipping, even small delays could have consequences.

The cargo discharge proceeded smoothly over the next two days, with gangs of stevedores working with professional efficiency to land their valuable freight. Elias supervised every aspect of the operation, knowing that his reputation for reliability depended on delivering cargo in perfect condition and on schedule.

It was on their third evening in port that Collins brought disturbing news.

"Captain," the young sailor approached with obvious reluctance, "there's been talk around the docks. American whalers asking questions about us, about our crew. The *Nantucket Queen* and her consorts are anchored in the lower pool."

Elias felt his jaw tighten. Captain Starbuck, it seemed, had not forgotten their Atlantic encounter and was planning some form of retaliation. In the rough world of London's waterfront, such things were often settled with fists rather than words.

"What sort of questions?"

"About when we're giving shore leave, sir. Which taverns our lads favor. How many of us there are." Collins paused, then added with the honesty that had always marked his character, "The boys are eager for it, sir. After what those whalers tried to pull at sea, they're spoiling for a proper fight."

It was exactly what Elias had feared. His crew's loyalty was absolute, but it also made them quick to take offense when their captain's honor was questioned. In the confined spaces of London's maritime district, a confrontation was probably inevitable.

"Very well," he decided. "Shore leave tonight for half the crew—port watch only. But they go in groups, stay together, and return by midnight. Any man who fails to report back forfeits his pay for the voyage."

Collins nodded eagerly. "Aye, sir. And if trouble finds us?"

"Then handle it like the men I know you are. But remember—you represent this ship and Nova Scotia. Whatever happens, conduct yourselves accordingly."

The Anchor and Chain was typical of London's sailor taverns—low-ceilinged, thick with pipe smoke, and filled with the kind of rough men who made their living from the sea's bounty. Santos, Murphy, Collins, and four other members of the *Intrepid's* crew had claimed a corner table, where they nursed their ale and swapped stories with the easy camaraderie of men who had shared danger and triumph.

The trouble started when a group of Americans entered, their weathered faces and purposeful stride marking them immediately as whalers. They surveyed the crowded taproom with the practiced eye of men looking for specific targets, and their gaze settled quickly on the Nova Scotians.

"Well, well," the largest of the Americans drawled, his voice carrying clearly over the tavern's din. "Look what we have here, boys. The brave colonial sailors who think they own the Atlantic Ocean."

Murphy looked up from his ale, his Irish eyes already beginning to smolder. "And good evening to you too, gentlemen. Though I don't believe we've been introduced."

"Name's Coffin," the big whaler replied, moving closer with obvious intent. "Boat steerer on the *Nantucket Queen*.

80

I hear you lads had some excitement with our captain a few weeks back."

"Excitement?" Santos spoke for the first time, his Portuguese accent thick with controlled anger. "Your captain, he tries to stop us on the high seas like pirate. Our captain, he shows him what real seamanship looks like."

The insult hit its mark perfectly. Coffin's face darkened, and his companions began spreading out in the unconscious formation of experienced brawlers. Around the tavern, other patrons sensed the building tension and began clearing space or moving toward the exits.

"Your captain's nothing but a lucky colonial with a fast ship," Coffin snarled. "And you're nothing but a bunch of timber haulers who wouldn't last five minutes in real weather."

That was the spark that ignited the powder keg. Murphy came up from his chair like a released spring, his fist connecting with Coffin's jaw with a sound like an ax striking wood. The big American staggered backward, crashed into another table, and sent its occupants scrambling for safety.

What followed was the kind of magnificent tavern brawl that would be talked about in London's maritime district for years to come. Santos grappled with two whalers simultaneously, his massive strength allowing him to literally lift one man off his feet and use him as a club against his companion. Collins, remembering lessons learned in Halifax's roughest neighborhoods, slipped under a roundhouse punch and delivered an uppercut that lifted a bearded harpooner completely off the floor.

Murphy danced through the chaos like a demon, his fists finding targets with mechanical precision while he sang snatches of fighting songs in Gaelic. Tables overturned, chairs flew through the air, and the tavern's collection of nautical bric-a-brac crashed to the floor in a symphony of destruction.

The end came suddenly when the constables arrived, their whistles shrieking and their truncheons ready. The fighting stopped as if by magic as both crews found themselves surrounded by London's finest, all of them breathing hard and sporting the kind of damage that spoke to a properly conducted brawl.

"Right then," the sergeant announced with the weary authority of a man who had broken up countless tavern fights, "you're all coming with us. The magistrate can sort out who did what to whom."

The Wapping Police Station stood like a fortress against the chaos of London's waterfront, its solid brick walls and iron-barred windows designed to contain the roughest elements of maritime society. Elias arrived there the following morning, having been summoned by a message that his crew was enjoying the hospitality of Her Majesty's government.

The desk sergeant, a grizzled veteran with the bearing of an old soldier, looked up from his paperwork with the expression of a man who had seen everything the docks could produce.

"Captain Johnson, I presume? Here about your lads?"

"Indeed I am, Sergeant. I trust they conducted themselves with appropriate dignity?"

The sergeant's snort suggested otherwise. "Dignity? Sir, they turned the Anchor and Chain into kindling and sent half a dozen American whalers to the surgery. Though I'll admit," he added with grudging respect, "they gave better than they got. Your boys can fight."

"What are the charges?"

"Disturbing the peace, destruction of property, assault and battery. The usual catalog of maritime sin. Magistrate's set bail at five pounds per man—forty pounds total for your crew."

It was a substantial sum but not unexpected. Elias had come prepared for such expenses, understanding that crew loyalty sometimes came with financial costs. He was counting out the money when a familiar voice interrupted the transaction.

"Well, if it isn't the brave Captain Johnson, come to rescue his crew from the consequences of their actions."

Elias turned to find Captain Starbuck standing behind him, the whaler's face showing the effects of whatever confrontation had brought him to the police station. A purple bruise decorated his left cheek, and his right hand was bandaged in a way that suggested damaged knuckles.

"Captain Starbuck. I trust your men are receiving appropriate medical attention?"

"They'll survive," Starbuck replied curtly. "Though I can't say the same for your reputation once word of this reaches the shipping offices. Brawling in taverns like common sailors—hardly the behavior expected of a ship's master."

It was a calculated insult, designed to provoke exactly the kind of reaction that would justify Starbuck's presence here. But Elias had not survived twenty-three years at sea by rising to every taunt, no matter how skillfully delivered.

"My men were defending their ship's honor," he said quietly. "Something I would have thought you'd understand, given your own profession's reputation for... direct action."

"Honor?" Starbuck's laugh was bitter as winter gale. "There's no honor in running from a fair fight at sea, then letting your crew do your fighting for you in port."

The accusation hung in the air between them like a challenge flag, and Elias felt something cold settle in his chest. Around them, the police station had grown quiet as clerks and constables sensed the building confrontation between the two sea captains.

"I never ran from anything in my life," Elias said, his voice carrying the absolute authority of command. "But if you feel the matter needs further settling, Captain Starbuck, I'm certainly available to discuss it."

It was Starbuck who moved first, his damaged hand swinging in a clumsy haymaker that telegraphed itself like a signal flag. Elias slipped the punch easily, his own fist connecting with the whaler's solar plexus in a blow that doubled the bigger man over with an explosive grunt.

The fight was brief and decisive. Starbuck, already weakened by whatever damage he had sustained the previous evening, proved no match for Elias's precise, economical boxing. Within moments, the whaler captain was on his knees, gasping for breath while Elias stood over him with his fists still raised.

"Gentlemen!" The desk sergeant's voice cut through the confrontation like a cutlass. "This is a police station, not a boxing ring! Captain Starbuck, I suggest you collect your men and depart before I decide to add you to our guest list. Captain Johnson, your crew's paperwork is ready."

Starbuck struggled to his feet, his face flushed with humiliation as well as pain. For a moment, Elias thought the man might try to continue the fight, but whatever fighting spirit had driven him this far finally collapsed under the weight of repeated defeat.

"This isn't over," he muttered, but the words carried no conviction.

"Yes, it is," Elias replied quietly. "Your quarrel was with me, not my crew. Now it's settled. Unless you want to make it a matter for the admiralty courts, I suggest we consider our business concluded."

The whaler captain's pale eyes held murder, but he was beaten and knew it. Without another word, he turned and stalked from the station, his dignity in tatters and his reputation severely damaged.

"Nicely done, sir," the sergeant observed as he completed the paperwork. "That one's been making trouble since he arrived in port. Good to see someone put him in his place."

An hour later, Elias stood on the *Intrepid's* deck watching his crew file aboard, their faces showing the mixed expression of men who had fought well and faced the consequences with proper dignity. They had proven themselves in the oldest and most direct way sailors knew, and their captain had finished what they had started.

"All accounted for, sir," Hartwell reported, though his grin suggested he knew more about the previous evening's events than his innocent expression indicated. "The lads are ready for duty, and eager to sail whenever you give the word."

"Very good, Mr. Hartwell. We'll complete loading this afternoon and clear for home tomorrow morning." Elias paused, then added with dry humor, "And perhaps we can manage the rest of our stay without further... diplomatic incidents."

The crew's laughter echoed across the docks, carrying with it the satisfaction of men who had faced their enemies and emerged victorious. They had settled their differences in the time-honored tradition of sailors throughout history, and their captain had proven himself worthy of their absolute loyalty in every way that mattered.

As the London evening settled over the Thames, the *Intrepid* rocked gently at her berth, her crew preparing for the homeward voyage with the quiet confidence of men who had proven themselves in battle. Whatever challenges awaited them on the Atlantic crossing, they would face them together, bound by the unbreakable bonds of shared triumph and mutual respect.

The whalers' humiliation was complete, and Captain Elias Johnson's reputation as a man not to be trifled with was now established throughout London's maritime community. It would be a story told in waterfront taverns for years to come—the night the Nova Scotian captain and his crew showed the American whalers what real fighting looked like.

Chapter 9: The Reckoning

The familiar outline of Yarmouth's harbor came into view on a gray October morning, the town's weathered buildings rising from the waterfront like old friends welcoming him home. Elias stood at the Intrepid's rail, watching the pilot boat approach through the light chop, and felt the satisfaction that always came with bringing his ship safely to port. The London voyage had been profitable—their holds were nearly empty, the cargo delivered on schedule despite the autumn gales that had plagued them through the Western Approaches.

"Fine landfall, Captain," Hartwell said, joining him at the rail. The young officer had grown more confident with each voyage, his navigation improving steadily under Elias's tutelage.

"Aye, she knows her way home." Elias nodded toward the approaching pilot boat. "That'll be old MacLeod coming out to us. Been piloting ships into this harbor since before you were born."

The pilot boat drew alongside with practiced precision, and MacLeod hauled himself up the Jacob's ladder with the agility of a man half his sixty-odd years. But when the grizzled pilot reached the deck, Elias noticed something different in his weathered face—a gravity that went beyond the usual concern for safe navigation.

"Morning, Captain Johnson," MacLeod said, accepting Elias's handshake. "Good to see the Intrepid home safe."

"Good to be home, Angus. How's the harbor treating you?"

MacLeod's eyes shifted uncomfortably. "Well enough, though there's changes coming. More steamers every month, fewer of the old sailing packets." He paused, studying Elias's face. "You haven't heard then, about Morrison & Company?"

A chill ran through Elias that had nothing to do with the October wind. "Heard what?"

"Best you speak with Mr. Morrison himself, Captain. I'll take her in."

The pilot's evasiveness only deepened Elias's unease. Throughout the careful navigation into Yarmouth's inner harbor, he found himself studying the waterfront with new attention. The changes were subtle but unmistakable— more steamships at the wharves, including several he didn't recognize. The forest of masts that had always characterized the harbor seemed thinner somehow, gaps where sailing ships should have been.

They made fast to Morrison & Company's private wharf, the same berth the Intrepid had occupied dozens of times before. But even here, something felt different. The usual bustle of stevedores and clerks seemed subdued, and Elias noticed several faces missing from the dock crew.

"Secure the ship, Mr. Hartwell," Elias ordered. "I'll be in the company offices."

"Aye, sir. Shall I begin discharge?"

"Wait on that. Let me speak with Mr. Morrison first."

The offices of Morrison & Company occupied a substantial brick building overlooking the harbor, its windows offering a commanding view of the shipping that was the lifeblood of Yarmouth's economy. Elias had climbed these stairs countless times over the years, first as a young officer reporting to the company's masters, later as a captain delivering his manifests and charts. The building felt like a second home.

But today, the familiar corridors seemed different. Several offices stood empty, their doors open to reveal vacant desks and bare walls where maritime charts had once hung. The usual sounds of commerce—clerks scratching in ledgers, the tick of the telegraph key, the bustle of men conducting the business of the sea—were muted, almost furtive.

He found Duncan Morrison in his corner office, the same room where Elias had received his first command nearly eight years ago. Morrison was bent over a stack of documents, his gray head moving slowly as he read. When he looked up at Elias's knock, his face showed the strain of a man wrestling with unwelcome decisions.

"Elias! Come in, come in." Morrison rose from behind his mahogany desk, but his usual hearty greeting lacked its customary warmth. "Good voyage, I trust?"

"Profitable and on schedule," Elias replied, settling into the leather chair across from Morrison's desk. "Though I get the feeling that's not the most pressing matter at hand."

Morrison's shoulders sagged slightly. "No, it's not." He moved to the window overlooking the harbor, his hands clasped behind his back. "How long have we done business together, Elias?"

"Near fifteen years, since I was second mate on the old Prosperity."

"Fifteen years. You've brought honor to this company, profit too. The Intrepid under your command has been one of our most reliable vessels." Morrison turned back to face him, his expression grave. "That's what makes this so damned difficult."

The chill Elias had felt on deck deepened into something approaching dread. "Makes what difficult?"

Morrison returned to his desk and picked up a thick document bound in blue legal paper. "Three weeks ago, I finalized the sale of Morrison & Company to the Atlantic Steam Navigation Company of Halifax."

The words hit Elias like a rogue wave. For a moment, he could only stare at the older man, trying to process what he'd heard. "Sold?"

"The steamers are taking over, Elias. Has been for years, but I've been too stubborn to admit it. They're faster, more reliable in terms of schedule. Passengers prefer them, and increasingly, so do shippers who need to know exactly when their goods will arrive." Morrison's voice carried the weariness of a man admitting defeat. "I've been hemorrhaging money for three years, trying to compete. The bank finally made it clear that I either sell or face bankruptcy."

"But the Intrepid's been profitable. All our London runs —"

"Profitable, yes, but not profitable enough. Atlantic Steam can move the same cargo in two-thirds the time, and they don't have to worry about being becalmed or fighting contrary winds." Morrison sat heavily in his chair. "They're keeping some of the vessels, converting them to steam auxiliary power. Others..." He spread his hands helplessly.

"Others?"

"Will be sold. The Intrepid among them."

Elias felt the deck shifting beneath him, though he knew the ship was firmly moored. His command, his beautiful barque that had carried him safely through countless voyages, to be sold like so much surplus gear. "And the captains? The crews?"

"Atlantic Steam is prepared to offer positions to qualified men willing to learn steam navigation. Starting positions, naturally. They have their own masters for their important routes."

"Starting positions." Elias's voice was flat. "You mean as junior officers."

Morrison nodded reluctantly. "The transition would be... difficult. But there would be work. Regular wages."

Elias rose from his chair and moved to the window, looking down at his ship. From this height, he could see Hartwell directing the crew in their end-of-voyage tasks, the familiar routine that had been the rhythm of his life for over two decades. Santos was checking the rigging, Murphy overseeing the younger hands. Men who had followed him through storms and calms, who trusted his judgment with their lives.

"What about my crew?"

"Those willing to transition to steam will be considered. The others..." Morrison's silence finished the sentence.

"When?"

"The transfer of ownership takes effect at the end of the month. You'll be expected to turn over the Intrepid to their representative on November first."

Three weeks. In three weeks, everything he had worked for, everything he had built, would pass into other hands. The command he had earned through skill and dedication, the trust of his men, the respect of the maritime community—all of it would be swept away by the relentless tide of technological progress.

"There is one other matter," Morrison continued quietly. "Atlantic Steam has asked me to recommend officers for their service. I've put forward your name, along with several others. Given your record, your reputation..."

"They'd consider me for what rank?"

Morrison's hesitation was answer enough. "Second officer, to start. On one of their coastal steamers. It's not what you deserve, Elias, but it's honest work. And there would be opportunity for advancement, given time."

Second officer. After commanding his own vessel, after years of carrying the ultimate responsibility for ship and crew, he was being offered a subordinate position on a steamer—a junior post he had held fifteen years ago. The irony was bitter as gall.

"I need time to think," Elias said finally.

"Of course. But don't take too long. They'll want an answer within the week, and there are other men seeking the same positions."

Elias turned from the window. Morrison's face showed genuine regret, and Elias realized that this conversation had been as difficult for the older man as it was for him. Duncan Morrison had built his company from nothing, had given dozens of young sailors their chance at command. Now he was watching his life's work dismantled by forces beyond his control.

"I understand your position, Duncan. You did what you had to do."

"I'm sorry, Elias. Truly sorry. If there was any other way..."

"There isn't. We both know that." Elias moved toward the door. "I'll give you my answer by week's end."

He left the building in a daze, the familiar sights and sounds of the waterfront seeming somehow distant and unreal. At the foot of the wharf, he paused to look back at the Intrepid. She sat proudly at her berth, her lines clean and purposeful, every inch the thoroughbred sailing ship. But now she seemed almost like a museum piece, a relic of an age that was passing even as he watched.

"Captain?" Hartwell's voice broke through his reverie. "Is everything all right, sir?"

Elias looked at the young officer—barely twenty-five, full of enthusiasm for the sea, believing as Elias once had that skill and dedication would always find their reward. How do you tell such a man that the world he's training for is disappearing beneath his feet?

"Carry on, Mr. Hartwell. We'll speak later."

The walk to his mother's house took him through the heart of Yarmouth, past the shops and warehouses that had grown prosperous on the sea trade. But even here, he noticed the signs of change. Several businesses had new

95

signs advertising services to steamship companies. A boilermaker's shop had opened where a sailmaker's loft once stood.

Margaret Johnson was in her garden when he arrived, tending to the late chrysanthemums that would soon succumb to the first hard frost. At sixty-one, she retained the upright bearing and sharp eyes that had carried her through widowhood and the challenges of raising a son alone. She looked up at his approach and smiled, but her expression quickly changed as she read his face.

"What's happened?"

"Morrison's sold the company. To a steam line."

She set down her garden shears and studied him with the penetrating gaze that had always been able to see through his boyhood attempts at deception. "And your command?"

"Gone. The Intrepid's to be sold."

For a long moment, they stood in the garden while the October wind rustled the dying leaves around them. Margaret had lived through the loss of her husband, had watched her son go to sea knowing the dangers he faced with every voyage. Now she was witnessing another kind of ending, the death of the world that had shaped their lives.

"What will you do?"

"They've offered me a berth. Second officer on a steamer."

"And?"

Elias looked toward the harbor, where the masts of the sailing ships stood silhouetted against the gray sky. "I don't know, Mother. I honestly don't know."

She moved closer and placed her hand on his arm. "Your father used to say that the sea gives with one hand and takes with the other. Perhaps this is just the sea's way of preparing you for something different."

"Or perhaps it's just the end of everything I've worked for."

"That's not the son I raised," she said firmly. "The son I raised never gave up when the tide turned against him. He found another way."

That evening, Elias walked the waterfront in the gathering dusk, trying to come to terms with the new reality. Other captains and officers moved through the familiar haunts— the shipping offices, the maritime insurance buildings, the taverns where sailors gathered to share news and gossip. But tonight, their conversations seemed subdued, marked by the same uncertainty that gripped him.

At the Anchor Tavern, he found several men he'd known for years, masters and mates from various sailing ships. The talk at their table was dominated by the same concern that consumed him.

"Heard about Morrison's company," said Captain Wright of the barque Seaventure. "Makes three local firms sold to steamship companies this year."

"It's happening everywhere," added Tom Fraser, first mate on the Highlander. "My cousin's up in Saint John says half the sailing packet lines there have either sold out or gone bankrupt."

"What about the West Indies trade?" Elias asked. "Surely there's still work there for sailing ships."

Wright shook his head grimly. "Competition's fierce. Too many vessels chasing too little cargo. And even there, steamers are making inroads. Met a man last week came back from Barbados, said the Royal Mail Steam Packet Company's got the passenger trade sewn up tight."

The conversation continued in this vein for another hour, each man sharing stories of companies sold, ships laid up, experienced officers scrambling for diminishing opportunities. When Elias finally left the tavern, he carried with him the sobering realization that his predicament was far from unique. Throughout the Maritime provinces, the same drama was playing out—the inexorable replacement of sail by steam, the end of an era that had defined their culture and economy for generations.

Standing at the end of the wharf where the Intrepid lay moored, Elias looked out at the harbor that had been his home port for most of his adult life. Tomorrow, he would have to face his crew and tell them that their world, like his, was about to change forever. Some would accept the transition to steam, learning new skills and adapting to new ways. Others, particularly the older hands, would find themselves adrift in a maritime world that no longer had use for their hard-won expertise.

But tonight, for just a little while longer, he could stand here and remember what it had been like to command his own vessel, to feel the deck alive beneath his feet as the Intrepid carved her way through Atlantic swells under a full press of canvas. Tomorrow would bring decisions and farewells, the dismantling of a life built around wind and tide and the eternal challenge of matching human skill against the moods of the sea.

The reckoning had come, as he'd always known it would. Now he had to decide how to face it.

Chapter 10: The Search

The first week of November brought an early snowfall to Yarmouth, the flakes swirling across the harbor like ashes from some great funeral pyre. Elias stood at his mother's kitchen window, watching the Intrepid's new owners prepare her for departure under steam power—the auxiliary engines that Atlantic Steam had hastily installed transforming his graceful barque into something alien and mechanical. Black smoke rose from her stack, staining the pristine canvas of her sails.

"You're going to wear a hole in that floor," Margaret observed from her chair by the fire, where she was mending one of his shirts.

Elias turned from the window, realizing he'd been pacing without conscious thought. "Sorry, Mother."

"Any word from Halifax?"

"Nothing promising." He picked up the latest letter from his writing desk—the fifth rejection in two weeks. "Captain Morrison of the barque Endeavour regrets to inform me that the position has been filled by an officer with twenty-two years' experience in command."

Twenty-two years. Against such seniority, Elias's eight years as master seemed almost negligible. What he'd thought was substantial experience now appeared modest compared to the veterans who were also scrambling for the diminishing number of sailing ship berths.

"Perhaps it's time to consider that position with Atlantic Steam," Margaret suggested gently.

The offer remained open—second officer on the coastal steamer Acadia. Regular wages, they'd emphasized. Steady work. But accepting would mean serving under men who might have far less sea time than he did, learning to tend machines instead of reading wind and weather.

"There are still possibilities, Mother. The West Indies trade, the lumber routes to South America. Steamers can't have taken everything."

Margaret's expression suggested she had little faith in these remaining possibilities, but she simply nodded and returned to her mending.

Over the following days, Elias threw himself into his search with increasing desperation. He wrote to every shipping agent from Halifax to Saint John, traveled to ports he'd previously considered beneath his notice, and swallowed his pride to approach companies he'd once dismissed as marginal operations.

The responses, when they came at all, followed a dispiriting pattern. The brigantine Celtic Queen, trading to Newfoundland, had given her command to Captain Horatio Blackwood—thirty years at sea, fifteen in command. The barque Wanderer, carrying lumber to Argentina, had selected Captain James MacLeod—veteran of twenty-six years, including service in the notorious guano trade to Peru. Even the ancient schooner

Persistence, running supplies to fishing stations, had gone to a man with eighteen years' command experience.

"It's not just about experience," Tom Fraser explained during one of his increasingly frequent visits. "It's about desperation. These old captains, men who've commanded fine ships for decades—they're willing to take anything rather than give up the sea entirely."

Fraser himself had been searching just as frantically, but for mate's berths rather than commands. Even there, the competition was fierce. First officers from prestigious lines were accepting second mate positions; second mates were shipping as bosuns. The entire hierarchy of sail was collapsing downward as too many qualified men chased too few opportunities.

"Captain Morrison of the Endeavour told me something interesting," Fraser continued. "He said he had over thirty applications for that position. Thirty captains, some with twice your sea time, willing to take command of a vessel that ten years ago would have been considered a step down for a senior mate."

The mathematics were cruel but undeniable. For every sailing ship command that became available, there were dozens of qualified masters seeking it. Age and seniority trumped competence when owners had their pick of experienced captains. Elias's specialization in the London trade, once a mark of distinction, now seemed like a liability—too refined for the rough-and-tumble coastal trades where sailing ships still found work.

December arrived with bitter winds and the kind of penetrating cold that made even heated rooms feel drafty. Elias's savings continued to dwindle. He'd been forced to let Hartwell and Santos go, unable to continue their partial wages. The young officer had found a berth as third mate on an Atlantic Steam vessel, while Santos had signed aboard a fishing schooner bound for the Grand Banks.

"At least they found work," Elias told his mother as they ate a sparse dinner of salt cod and potatoes.

"And so could you, if you'd swallow that stubborn pride of yours."

The argument that had been simmering between them for weeks finally boiled over. "It's not just pride, Mother. If I take that steamship berth, I'm admitting defeat. I'm saying that everything I've learned, everything I've worked for, means nothing."

"And if you don't take it, what then? Will you let us both starve rather than admit the world has changed?"

Her words stung because they carried uncomfortable truth. His savings would last perhaps another month, two at the most. Margaret's small pension and the income from her garden covered basic expenses, but not much more. Pride might be a luxury, as she'd said, but poverty was a harsh master that brooked no argument.

The next morning brought a letter that seemed to offer hope—an inquiry from Caldwell & Associates of Halifax regarding command of the coastal trader Morning Star.

Elias caught the first available transport to Halifax, his spirits higher than they'd been in weeks.

Caldwell's office was cramped and redolent of coal smoke, but the agent seemed genuinely interested in Elias's qualifications. The Morning Star was a small barquentine, he explained, engaged in carrying general cargo between Maritime ports and occasionally to Boston or New York.

"She's not much to look at," Caldwell admitted, "but she's sound. The previous captain decided to try his luck in the United States, left rather suddenly. We need someone who can take command immediately."

The terms were modest—less than half what Elias had earned on the Intrepid—but they represented steady employment and the chance to remain in sail. More importantly, Caldwell seemed impressed by Elias's record and spoke as if the position was his for the taking.

"When can I see the vessel?" Elias asked.

"Well, there's just one small matter to settle first. Another candidate has expressed interest—Captain Augustus Brennan. Perhaps you know him? He's had command of several vessels in the Caribbean trade, quite experienced..."

The name hit Elias like a physical blow. Not Brennan the Third Mate he'd known, surely, but the surname was uncommon enough to make coincidence unlikely. His suspicion was confirmed when Caldwell produced a letter of recommendation.

"Yes, Captain Brennan," Caldwell continued, consulting the letter. "Twenty-one years at sea, eight in various commands. Most recently master of the barque Perseverance in the molasses trade. Very impressive credentials."

Eight years in command—exactly matching Elias's own experience, but Brennan's sea time stretched back further. If this was indeed the same man who'd served under him as Third Mate, he'd clearly made up for lost time since leaving the Providence.

"Has Captain Brennan seen the vessel yet?" Elias asked carefully.

"He arrives tomorrow morning. I thought it best to interview both candidates before making a decision." Caldwell's tone had grown noticeably cooler, suggesting that Brennan's superior credentials had already made an impression.

Elias left Halifax that afternoon knowing he'd lost another opportunity before he'd even had a fair chance at it. The irony was bitter—if this was indeed his former subordinate, Brennan would be getting commands while Elias was reduced to begging for them.

January brought no relief. Letter after letter yielded the same results: positions filled by more senior men, or requirements for experience Elias didn't possess. A schooner captain was needed for the lumber trade—but they wanted someone familiar with South American ports.

A barque required a master for the sugar islands—but experience in the Caribbean was essential. Each rejection seemed calculated to remind him that his specialization, once a source of pride, had become a prison.

By February, even Tom Fraser had given up the search. "Found a berth as bosun on a fishing vessel," he announced during his final visit before departing for the Banks. "It's not much, but it's work. My wife's tired of counting pennies."

"What about the Celtic Queen? I thought MacPherson was looking for a master."

Fraser shook his head. "Went to Captain Blackwood last month. Man's got twenty-eight years at sea, fifteen in command. Even offered to take a cut in salary just to stay in sail."

Alone now in his search, Elias made increasingly desperate trips to Saint John, Shelburne, Lunenburg—any port that might still harbor sailing vessels in need of masters. But everywhere the story was the same. The few remaining positions went to men whose credentials dwarfed his own, captains who'd commanded ships when he was still learning to splice rope.

At a shipping office in Saint John, he encountered one such veteran—Captain William MacLeod, a weathered man in his sixties who'd spent forty years at sea, twenty-five in command.

"You're young yet," MacLeod told him kindly. "Take that steamship berth while you can. This"—he gestured toward the nearly empty harbor—"this is finished. Oh, there'll be a few sailing ships left for years to come, carrying cargo too cheap for steam or serving ports too small to matter. But they'll be commanded by old fools like me who don't know how to do anything else."

"You could learn steam," Elias suggested.

MacLeod laughed bitterly. "At my age? They want young men who can adapt, who won't resent the new ways. Men like you, Captain Johnson. Don't make the mistake of thinking you have to go down with this particular ship."

Walking back to his lodgings through Saint John's snowy streets, Elias passed the offices of several steamship companies. Electric lights blazed in their windows despite the early hour, illuminating clerks and agents managing the complex logistics of steam navigation. Their world ran on schedules and timetables, on the predictable rhythm of mechanical power rather than the ancient dance between wind and sail.

The next morning, he composed two letters. The first was to Atlantic Steam Navigation Company, accepting their offer of a second officer's berth on the steamer Acadia. The second was to his mother, explaining his decision in words that tried to mask his sense of defeat.

The reply came within a week—a brief, businesslike note instructing him to report to the Acadia's First Officer in

Halifax on March 15th for orientation. The letter was signed by the Marine Superintendent, but a handwritten note at the bottom caught his attention:

"Looking forward to serving with you again, Johnson. —J. Brennan, First Officer."

So it was true. His former Third Mate, the man he'd passed over for promotion in favor of Hartwell, would now be his superior officer. The wheel of fortune had made a complete revolution, carrying Brennan up even as it brought Elias down.

That evening, sitting by the fire in his mother's parlor, Elias stared at the letter until the words blurred. Eight years of command, eight years of responsibility and respect, reduced to this—reporting as a subordinate to a man who'd once taken orders from him.

"You're doing the right thing," Margaret said quietly, though her voice carried no conviction.

"Am I? Or am I just giving up?"

"You're surviving. That's what your father would have done."

Perhaps she was right. Perhaps survival was its own form of victory in a world that no longer valued the skills he'd spent his life perfecting. But as he folded the letter and placed it on the mantel, Elias couldn't escape the feeling that he was attending his own funeral—burying Captain

Johnson to make way for Second Officer Johnson, a lesser man in a diminished world.

Outside, the March wind howled around the house like a banshee keening for the dead. In six days, he would board a steamship not as a passenger or visitor, but as a member of her crew. The thought filled him with a dread deeper than any storm he'd ever weathered.

Chapter 11: Reporting Aboard

The steamship Acadia lay moored at Halifax's Pier 21, her black hull gleaming with fresh paint and her single funnel rising stark against the gray March sky. She was a handsome vessel in her way—240 feet of modern efficiency, built for the coastal passenger and freight trade that had become the backbone of Maritime commerce. But to Elias, approaching her gangway with his sea bag over his shoulder, she might as well have been a floating prison.

The morning was crisp, with the kind of biting wind that promised winter's last stand before yielding to spring. Other members of the crew were boarding ahead of him— deckhands carrying their gear, a junior engineer with oil-stained overalls, passengers bound for Saint John clutching their traveling bags. All moved with the casual confidence of people who belonged in this mechanized world.

Elias paused at the foot of the gangway, studying the vessel that would be his new home. Her lines were clean and purposeful, designed for speed and economy rather than the graceful beauty of sail. Twin paddle wheels dominated her midsection, their housings painted white to match her superstructure. Steam wisped from various vents and fittings, giving her the appearance of a beast barely contained.

"Well, well. Second Officer Johnson, I presume?"

The voice carried unmistakable malice wrapped in false civility. Elias turned to find James Brennan approaching from the direction of the ship's offices, dressed in the dark blue uniform of the Atlantic Steam Navigation Company. The years had hardened him—his frame had filled out with the solid bearing of command, but his face bore the cold satisfaction of a man savoring long-awaited revenge. His eyes glittered with barely contained hostility.

"Mr. Brennan." Elias managed to keep his voice level. "Or should I say, First Officer Brennan?"

"You'll address me as 'Mister Brennan' or 'sir,' Johnson. We're not shipmates anymore—I'm your superior officer now." The smile was cold as winter steel. "Amazing how things change, isn't it? The great Captain Johnson, reduced to taking orders from his former Third Mate."

The message was clear enough. Whatever their past relationship, Brennan now held the superior position and intended to use it. Elias nodded curtly and shouldered his bag.

"Shall we get aboard then? I'm eager to learn my duties."

Brennan led the way up the gangway, his stride deliberately slow, forcing Elias to follow like a subordinate. "She's a fine vessel, the Acadia. Modern. Efficient. Nothing like those obsolete sailing coffins you used to command. Those days are finished, Johnson—and so are the men who couldn't adapt."

111

They crossed the deck, past the paddle wheel housings toward the deckhouse that contained the officers' quarters. The deck was spotless, painted in alternating strips of white and blue, with brass fittings that gleamed despite the overcast sky. Everything spoke of mechanical precision, of systems designed to function regardless of weather or season.

"Your cabin's here," Brennan said, opening a door marked "Second Officer." "Cramped, isn't it? Nothing like the spacious quarters you enjoyed as master of the mighty Intrepid. But then, you're not a captain anymore, are you? Just another junior officer learning his trade."

The cabin was indeed small—barely eight feet square, with a narrow bunk, a compact writing desk, and space for a single sea chest. Brennan stood in the doorway, deliberately blocking the entrance while Elias waited with his sea bag.

"Of course, if you find the accommodations... inadequate... I'm sure you could find work ashore. Perhaps as a dock foreman? I hear they pay well for men who can count cargo." His laugh was harsh. "Ten minutes on the bridge, Johnson. And don't keep me waiting—punctuality is essential in steam service."

Alone in his cabin, Elias stowed his possessions in the limited storage space. His sextant, compass, and other navigational instruments seemed almost anachronistic here, where steam power made precise celestial navigation less critical than understanding mechanical systems and coal consumption rates. He changed into his new uniform —the blue serge and brass buttons of Atlantic Steam—and studied himself in the small mirror mounted above the washbasin.

The face that looked back at him was still recognizably his own, but something fundamental had changed. Where once he'd worn the quiet confidence of command, now he saw the careful neutrality of a subordinate. At thirty-seven, he was starting over in a profession that no longer valued his hardest-won skills.

The bridge of the Acadia occupied the top of her deckhouse, offering a commanding view of the harbor and surrounding cityscape. It was smaller than the quarterdeck of a sailing ship but equipped with instruments that would have seemed magical a generation earlier—telegraph to the engine room, steam steering gear, electric communication with various parts of the vessel.

Captain Morrison was a compact man in his fifties, with the quick movements and sharp eyes of someone accustomed to making rapid decisions in confined spaces. He looked up from a chart as Elias approached, his expression neutral but appraising.

"So you're Johnson. Brennan tells me you've had command of sailing vessels."

"Yes, sir. Most recently the barque Intrepid, London trade."

"Good record, from what I hear. Unfortunate about Morrison & Company, but these things happen. The important thing now is adapting to steam." Morrison's tone was matter-of-fact, neither sympathetic nor dismissive. "This isn't like sail, Johnson. We run to schedules, not weather. Passengers expect to arrive when we say we will, regardless of wind or tide."

"I understand, sir."

"Do you? We'll see." Morrison gestured toward the engine room telegraph. "Your primary responsibility will be cargo and passenger manifest, but you'll also need to understand our mechanical systems. Can't have an officer who doesn't know the difference between the main engine and the donkey boiler."

For the next hour, Brennan conducted a tour that felt more like a public humiliation. They visited the engine room, where massive pistons drove the paddle wheels with mechanical precision; the passenger saloons, appointed with mahogany and brass fixtures; the cargo holds, designed for rapid loading.

At each location, Brennan posed questions clearly designed to expose Elias's ignorance. "How long to raise steam from cold, Johnson? No idea? Surprising, for such an experienced mariner." His voice dripped with false concern. "What's normal boiler pressure? Don't know that either? Dear me. How do you calculate coal consumption? Still drawing a blank?"

114

When Elias admitted his unfamiliarity with the systems, Brennan's explanations were deliberately condescending, delivered in the tone one might use with a slow child. "It's quite simple, really. Even ordinary deckhands pick it up quickly. But then, they haven't spent years believing that ancient superstitions about wind and weather make them superior to honest working men."

"There now," Brennan said as they concluded the tour near the passenger gangway. "Not so mysterious after all, is it? Steam is the future, Johnson—reliable, predictable, profitable. Unlike all that romantic nonsense about reading the wind and communing with the sea." His laugh was deliberately loud, drawing curious glances from nearby crew members. "Though I suppose some men are too set in their ways to learn new tricks. Too proud to admit their skills are worthless."

The implied comparison was unmistakable. Sail required skill and experience; steam was merely a matter of following procedures. It was a view Elias had encountered repeatedly during his job search—the assumption that mechanical systems were inherently simpler than the ancient art of working with wind and weather.

Their first voyage departed Halifax at precisely two o'clock, as advertised in the company's published schedule. Elias stood on the bridge wing, watching the harbor slide past as the Acadia's paddle wheels churned through the dark water. There was something undeniably impressive about the vessel's steady progress, her ability to maintain course and speed regardless of the light headwind that would have made this a long beat to windward under sail.

But there was also something missing—the subtle interplay between ship and sea that had defined his professional life. The Acadia moved through the water rather than with it, imposing her will through mechanical force rather than finding harmony with natural elements. She was efficient, reliable, profitable—everything that mattered to the commercial world that had replaced sail. Yet to Elias, she felt fundamentally disconnected from the sea that carried her.

"Impressive, isn't she?" Captain Morrison had joined him at the rail. "Built in Glasgow three years ago, latest design. Can make the run to Saint John in eight hours regardless of weather, carry forty passengers in comfort and a hundred tons of freight."

"She's certainly fast," Elias agreed.

"Fast and dependable. That's what passengers pay for—knowing they'll arrive on schedule, not when the wind happens to be favorable." Morrison studied Elias's expression. "You're thinking this is all very mechanical, very removed from real seamanship. Most sailing ship men do, initially."

"The thought had occurred to me."

"Let me tell you something, Johnson. Running a steamship on schedule, in all weather, serving ports where minutes

116

matter—that takes seamanship too. Different skills, perhaps, but no less demanding. The sea doesn't care whether you're driven by wind or steam. She'll test you either way."

Morrison's words carried conviction, but Elias remained unconvinced. The Acadia's progress felt too easy, too divorced from the eternal struggle between human skill and natural forces that had made sailing such a demanding art. Here, skill lay in managing machines rather than reading weather, in maintaining schedules rather than seizing opportunities offered by wind and tide.

As if summoned by these thoughts, Brennan appeared at his elbow. "Captain's asked me to show you the passenger manifest. Part of your duties will be ensuring their comfort and safety."

They descended to the main saloon, where passengers were settling in for the voyage to Saint John. The accommodations were indeed impressive—upholstered seats, polished woodwork, large windows offering panoramic views of the passing coastline. A steward moved among the travelers, serving tea and small cakes with the practiced efficiency of hotel service.

"Twenty-six passengers this trip," Brennan said, making a show of consulting his manifest while speaking loudly enough for nearby passengers to hear. "All expecting professional service from competent officers. The gentleman by the window is Mr. Patterson—owns textile mills in Saint John. He values punctuality and reliability,

117

traits that steamship officers possess." His voice grew pointed. "Not like those sailing ship captains who used to arrive days late, blaming the weather for their incompetence."

It struck Elias that this level of personal attention would have been impossible aboard a sailing packet, where passengers were generally left to their own devices once they'd paid their fare. Steam service, with its regular schedules and predictable conditions, had transformed ocean travel into something resembling railway transport —scheduled, comfortable, reliable.

But the human cost of this transformation was evident in Brennan's systematic cruelty. There was vicious satisfaction in how he corrected each small mistake, a need to publicly humiliate that went far beyond professional duty. His years under competent commanders had taught him the forms of leadership, but they had also nurtured the resentments that now drove his petty tyranny.

"Everything seems... efficient," Elias said carefully, aware that several passengers were listening.

"Efficient. Professional. Modern." Brennan's voice carried deliberate emphasis on each word. "Everything the old sailing service never was. But don't concern yourself with such matters, Johnson—your job is to follow orders and try not to embarrass the company. Think you can manage that, or shall I find someone more... capable?"

The condescension was impossible to miss, but Elias forced himself to remain silent. This was his reality now—taking instruction from a man who had once deferred to his judgment, accepting diminished status in a world that valued mechanical efficiency over maritime skill.

That evening, as the Acadia approached Saint John through the gathering dusk, Elias stood on the bridge wing and watched the familiar coastline slide past. The lights of the city were beginning to twinkle in the darkness, welcoming another steamship arrival to a harbor increasingly dominated by vessels like theirs.

Behind him, he could hear Captain Morrison discussing tomorrow's schedule with Brennan—departure at six sharp, stops at three intermediate ports, arrival in Halifax precisely at four in the afternoon. It was all very orderly, very predictable, very profitable.

But as the Acadia's paddle wheels churned steadily through the dark water, Elias couldn't escape the feeling that something essential had been lost in this triumph of mechanical precision. The sea had been reduced to a highway, ships to carriages following predetermined routes. Where once there had been adventure, now there was only schedule.

"Quite a change from the old days, eh Johnson?" Brennan's voice carried cold satisfaction as he savored his former captain's reduced circumstances. "Remember when you used to strut around your quarterdeck, playing God with wind and weather? All that arrogance, all that precious 'seamanship.'" He spat the word like a curse. "This is the real world now—schedules, efficiency, profit. No room for washed-up sailing masters who think they're something special."

Elias turned to face his former subordinate, seeing in his expression not just satisfaction but active malice—the vindictive pleasure of a man finally able to repay years of perceived slights. For Brennan, the steamship represented more than employment; it was the perfect weapon for revenge against the man who had once passed him over for promotion.

"Indeed," Elias replied quietly, his voice carefully neutral. "Very... modern."

"Oh, it's more than modern, Johnson. It's justice." Brennan's smile was cruel. "All those years watching you hand promotions to your favorites, listening to everyone praise the great Captain Johnson. Now look at you— taking orders from your former Third Mate, learning like a common apprentice." He leaned closer, his voice dropping to a venomous whisper. "And this is just the beginning."

But as he spoke the words, he felt something die within him—some essential part of his identity that had been bound up with the challenge of matching human skill against the unpredictable forces of wind and sea. Tomorrow would bring another scheduled run, another exercise in mechanical efficiency.

And he would play his part, the experienced sailing master learning to tend machines under the supervision of his former Third Mate. It was, he supposed, a kind of justice —the wheel of fortune completing its revolution, carrying him down as it lifted others up.

But it felt very much like defeat.

Chapter 12: Steam and Spite

The next three weeks aboard the Acadia fell into a pattern of systematic humiliation that Brennan orchestrated with the precision of a master tactician. Each day brought fresh indignities, new ways to remind Elias of his diminished status while teaching him the bitter lesson that revenge, like steam pressure, built slowly but inexorably toward explosion.

It began with the duty roster. Where other officers worked standard watches, Brennan assigned Elias to the most inconvenient hours—midnight to four in the morning, then again from noon to four in the afternoon. The split schedule made proper rest impossible and ensured that Elias was perpetually exhausted, stumbling through his duties while Brennan watched with undisguised satisfaction.

"Something wrong with your watch schedule, Johnson?" Brennan asked during their third day out from Halifax, his voice carrying across the bridge loud enough for Captain Morrison to hear. "You seem... tired. Perhaps steamship service is too demanding for men of your advanced years?"

Elias bit back his response, knowing that any complaint would only provide Brennan with fresh ammunition. At thirty-seven, he was hardly elderly, but the irregular sleep and constant stress were beginning to show in the shadows beneath his eyes, the slight tremor in his hands when fatigue overtook him.

The harassment extended beyond mere scheduling. Brennan delighted in assigning Elias the most menial tasks —scrubbing the passenger deck on his hands and knees while first-class travelers stepped around him, polishing brass fittings that gleamed perfectly already, inventorying cargo holds that had been checked twice before. Work that would normally be delegated to ordinary seamen became "essential training" for the former sailing master.

"Experience with honest labor will do you good," Brennan announced during one such assignment, loud enough for a group of passengers to overhear. "Too many sailing ship captains think themselves above real work. Time you learned what the men under your command actually did."

The worst part was Brennan's systematic campaign to undermine Elias's credibility with both crew and passengers. He would wait until Elias made some minor error—mispronouncing the name of a mechanical component, hesitating over an unfamiliar procedure—then pounce with theatrical concern.

"Oh dear, Johnson. Surely you know the difference between the main condenser and the feed pump? No? How... unfortunate. Mr. Collins, perhaps you could explain to our Second Officer how steam condensation works?"

The junior engineer, clearly uncomfortable with being used as a weapon in this personal war, would mumble an explanation while Elias stood silent, his face burning with shame. Each such incident was witnessed by crew members or passengers, slowly building a reputation for incompetence that Brennan nurtured with malicious care.

But it was in the engine room that Brennan's vindictiveness reached its cruelest heights. The domain of Chief Engineer MacReady was a temple of mechanical precision, where massive pistons drove the paddle wheels with rhythmic thunder and steam hissed through a maze of pipes and valves. For a man raised on wind and sail, it was an alien environment filled with dangers both obvious and subtle.

"Second Officer Johnson needs to understand our propulsion systems," Brennan announced to MacReady during Elias's second week aboard. "I'm placing him under your supervision for engine room training. I trust you'll be... thorough."

MacReady was a decent man, worn down by years of coaxing maximum performance from temperamental machinery. He took his teaching duties seriously, patiently explaining the intricacies of boiler pressure, cylinder temperatures, and coal consumption rates. But Brennan made sure to appear whenever Elias was struggling with some particularly complex concept.

"Still having trouble with thermal efficiency calculations?" Brennan would inquire with false sympathy. "Perhaps we should start with simpler mathematics? Addition and subtraction, perhaps?"

The engine room work was genuinely dangerous. Steam at high pressure could scald flesh from bone in seconds, while moving machinery could crush a careless hand without hesitation. Elias approached each task with the careful attention that had kept him alive through countless storms, but exhaustion made concentration difficult and unfamiliarity bred uncertainty.

It was during his third week that disaster nearly struck. Brennan had assigned him to assist with boiler maintenance—checking water levels and adjusting pressure valves while the engines operated at cruise power. The work required precise timing and absolute attention to gauge readings, but Elias had been on duty since midnight and fatigue clouded his judgment.

"Pressure's running high in number two boiler," MacReady called out over the engine noise. "Ease off the main valve, Johnson—slowly now!"

Elias reached for what he thought was the correct valve, but confusion over the complex array of controls made him hesitate. In that moment of uncertainty, Brennan appeared at his shoulder.

"Problem, Johnson? Surely such a simple task isn't beyond your capabilities?" His voice was loud enough to carry over the engine noise, ensuring that several nearby stokers witnessed the exchange. "Or perhaps you'd prefer to return to your cabin and let competent men handle this?"

The taunt broke Elias's concentration completely. He grabbed for the nearest valve, turning it in what he hoped was the correct direction, but the gauge needle climbed instead of falling. Steam pressure in the boiler soared past safe limits while warning whistles began to shriek.

"Wrong valve!" MacReady roared, diving past Elias to reach the emergency release. "Stand clear!"

Superheated steam erupted from the safety valve with a sound like artillery fire, filling the engine room with scalding vapor that sent everyone scrambling for cover. For a terrifying moment, the entire boiler system teetered on the edge of catastrophic failure before MacReady's skilled hands brought it back under control.

In the sudden silence that followed, every face in the engine room turned toward Elias. Some showed concern, others confusion, but all reflected the same realization— the Second Officer had nearly destroyed the ship's power plant through simple incompetence.

"Well," Brennan said into the silence, his voice carrying theatrical dismay. "That was... educational. Perhaps engine room work is too complex for men trained only in obsolete technologies?"

MacReady's face was grim as he surveyed the damage— blown gaskets, twisted piping, gauges knocked off their calibrations by the pressure surge. "Two hours minimum to make repairs," he announced. "We'll have to reduce to half power until I can get the system properly balanced."

Captain Morrison appeared within minutes, summoned by reports of the emergency. His expression grew darker as he surveyed the scene, taking in the damaged equipment and the obvious cause of the problem.

"Explain," he said simply.

Brennan stepped forward with every appearance of reluctant duty. "Training accident, sir. Mr. Johnson was attempting to adjust boiler pressure when he... miscalculated. Mr. MacReady's quick action prevented serious damage, but we'll need to make repairs before proceeding at full power."

Morrison's gaze shifted to Elias, who stood silent amid the wreckage of his dignity. There was disappointment in the captain's eyes, but also something like understanding—the look of a man who recognized the signs of systematic persecution but felt powerless to address it directly.

"Report to my cabin in one hour, Johnson. We need to discuss your training progress."

The interview was brief but devastating. Morrison made no direct accusations, but his message was clear— steamship service required absolute precision, and officers who couldn't maintain proper standards endangered the entire vessel. Elias found himself demoted to the most basic duties, effectively removed from any position where his inexperience might cause further damage.

"This isn't personal, Johnson," Morrison said, though his tone suggested he understood exactly how personal it had become. "But I can't risk the ship or passengers on good intentions. You'll continue your training under Mr. Brennan's supervision, but with... closer oversight."

Closer oversight meant constant surveillance. Brennan now shadowed Elias's every move, correcting his smallest mistakes with theatrical patience while ensuring that crew and passengers witnessed each humiliation. The pretense of training became a public exhibition of incompetence, designed to destroy not just Elias's position but his reputation throughout the Maritime shipping community.

"Careful with that manifest, Johnson," Brennan would announce when Elias struggled with unfamiliar cargo notations. "We wouldn't want another... miscalculation. Perhaps you should let someone more qualified handle the mathematics?"

The psychological toll was as exhausting as the physical demands. Elias found himself second-guessing every decision, hesitating over tasks that should have been routine. Sleep became elusive, haunted by nightmares of exploding boilers and crushing machinery. His appetite disappeared, leaving him gaunt and hollow-eyed, the very image of defeat that Brennan had worked so carefully to create.

But perhaps the cruelest aspect of Brennan's campaign was how he used Elias's own competence against him. When passengers asked about maritime matters—weather patterns, navigation techniques, the history of Atlantic shipping—Brennan would defer to his subordinate with false generosity.

"Mr. Johnson here was once a sailing ship captain," he would announce with apparent admiration. "Perhaps he could share some stories of the old days? I'm sure our passengers would enjoy hearing about... traditional methods."

The resulting conversations were exercises in humiliation disguised as courtesy. Passengers would listen politely to Elias's explanations of celestial navigation or wind patterns, then turn to Brennan with questions about modern steamship efficiency. The contrast was always the same—romantic but obsolete knowledge versus practical contemporary expertise.

"Fascinating how they used to do things," one businessman commented after Elias explained the principles of dead reckoning. "Thank goodness for steam power and proper scheduling. One knows exactly when one will arrive."

As the Acadia completed her regular circuit between Halifax, Saint John, and the smaller coastal ports, Elias realized that Brennan's revenge extended beyond personal satisfaction. He was systematically destroying any possibility that Elias might find better employment, ensuring that word of his incompetence would spread throughout the Maritime shipping community. No captain would want an officer who had nearly destroyed a boiler through carelessness. No company would trust a man who couldn't handle basic steamship procedures.

The trap was perfectly constructed. Each mistake, each humiliation, each public failure was carefully witnessed and would be duly reported when the Acadia reached port. Brennan was not merely punishing his former captain—he was ensuring that this punishment would be permanent, that Elias would never again find employment worthy of his skills.

Standing on the deck during a brief moment of solitude, watching the familiar Nova Scotia coastline slide past under gray April skies, Elias understood that he was witnessing the death of more than just his career. Brennan was methodically destroying the man who had once commanded the Intrepid, replacing him with a broken subordinate who embodied everything that traditional seamanship had become—obsolete, incompetent, irrelevant.

The question that haunted him was whether anything of the real Elias Johnson would survive this systematic destruction. Each day brought fresh proof of his inadequacy, each failure reinforced Brennan's narrative of inevitable decline. Soon, even he might begin to believe that his years of successful command had been nothing more than luck, that his skills were truly as worthless as Brennan proclaimed.

But somewhere beneath the exhaustion and humiliation, a spark of the old determination still flickered. He had survived storms that would have crushed lesser men, had brought ships safely through perils that claimed other vessels. Brennan might have superior position and mechanical knowledge, but he had never possessed the essential qualities that made a true seaman.

The test would come—it always did. And when it did, they would learn whether experience and seamanship were truly obsolete, or whether the sea still recognized the difference between competence and mere authority.

Until then, he could only endure, and hope that endurance would prove to be enough.

Chapter 13: Dead in the Water

The barometer had been falling steadily for three days as the Acadia made her way north from Saint John toward Halifax, but Captain Morrison seemed unconcerned. The steamship's published schedule called for arrival at four in the afternoon, and steam power made such precision possible regardless of weather conditions. Why worry about wind and sea when mechanical force could overcome both?

Elias watched the weather signs with growing unease. The high, thin clouds of Tuesday had thickened into the gray overcast of Wednesday, while the wind had backed from southwest to southeast and begun to strengthen. The sea, which had been running in long, lazy swells, now showed whitecaps that grew more numerous with each passing hour. Every instinct developed over twenty-three years at sea warned him that a serious blow was building.

But his warnings carried no weight aboard a steamship commanded by men who believed mechanical power had made weather irrelevant. When he mentioned his concerns to Brennan during the morning watch, his superior officer responded with predictable contempt.

"Worried about a little wind, Johnson? I suppose that's natural for someone raised on sailing ships." Brennan's voice carried across the bridge, ensuring that the quartermaster and lookout witnessed this latest humiliation. "Those of us who understand modern navigation don't need to cower every time the weather turns unpleasant."

Captain Morrison, when approached directly, was more polite but equally dismissive. "The glass is dropping, certainly, but nothing our engines can't handle. We've weathered worse storms than this without difficulty. Steam power gives us options that sailing vessels never possessed."

By noon on Thursday, those options were beginning to seem less certain. The wind had increased to force six, driving spray across the Acadia's bridge and sending green water over her bow. The passenger saloon, normally filled with comfortable travelers, now echoed with the sounds of seasickness as the steamship pitched and rolled through increasingly heavy seas.

But it was the subtle changes in the engine room that first told Elias the real story. The steady rhythm of the paddle wheels, which had provided such reassuring certainty during calm weather, now stuttered and faltered as the ship's motion lifted them partially clear of the water. Steam consumption soared as the engines worked harder to maintain speed against mounting headwinds, while coal consumption rates climbed far beyond normal parameters.

"Pressure's running low in the starboard boiler," MacReady reported to Brennan during the afternoon watch. "The motion's affecting our draft, and we're burning coal faster than I can shovel it."

Brennan waved away the engineer's concerns with characteristic arrogance. "Maintain schedule, MacReady. The passengers expect to reach Halifax on time."

But by evening, even Brennan couldn't ignore the mounting evidence that the Acadia was fighting a losing battle against the storm. What had begun as an inconvenient headwind had developed into a full gale, with seas running fifteen feet and spray freezing on the rigging as temperatures dropped. The steamship, designed for coastal service in moderate conditions, was being pushed beyond her limits by forces that recognized no distinction between sail and steam.

Elias was attempting to secure loose cargo in the forward hold when the first real crisis struck. A tremendous sea crashed over the bow, sending water cascading through the passenger deck and into the cargo spaces below. But worse than the flooding was the sound that accompanied it—a grinding, metallic shriek from the engine room that spoke of machinery pushed past its breaking point.

He found MacReady and his assistants working frantically over the starboard engine, steam hissing from fractured pipes while warning bells clanged throughout the compartment. The chief engineer's face was grim as he surveyed the damage.

"Connecting rod's cracked," MacReady shouted over the noise of escaping steam. "Been working too hard in these heavy seas. We'll have to shut down the starboard engine before she destroys herself completely."

The loss of half her power transformed the Acadia from a confident steamship into a vessel barely able to maintain steerage way. Captain Morrison, summoned to the engine room by the emergency bells, stared at the disabled machinery with the expression of a man watching his certainties crumble.

"How long for repairs?" he asked.

MacReady shook his head grimly. "In these conditions? Can't be done, sir. That connecting rod needs to be pulled and machined, work that requires calm seas and proper tools. Best I can do is seal off the damaged cylinder and hope the port engine holds together."

With only one engine functioning, the Acadia's speed dropped to barely four knots—insufficient to make headway against the mounting gale. Morrison ordered a course change, attempting to run for the shelter of the nearest harbor, but even this modest goal seemed increasingly beyond their reach as the storm continued to intensify.

By midnight, the situation had deteriorated from serious to desperate. The remaining engine, forced to work at maximum power to maintain any forward motion at all, began showing signs of strain. Steam pressure fluctuated wildly as the ship's motion affected boiler efficiency, while the constant pounding stressed every component beyond its design limits.

"She's shaking herself apart," MacReady reported during a brief lull between the worst seas. "That port engine's doing the work of two, and she wasn't built for it. If she fails, we'll be completely dead in the water."

It was then that the unthinkable happened. A rogue wave, larger than any that had preceded it, caught the Acadia as she struggled up the face of a particularly steep sea. The impact drove her bow deep into the trough beyond, burying her paddle wheels completely and subjecting the remaining engine to stresses it was never designed to handle.

The port connecting rod, already weakened by hours of excessive strain, finally succumbed with a sound like artillery fire. Steam erupted from ruptured pipes as the massive piston locked solid, bringing the paddle wheels to a grinding halt that left the Acadia wallowing helplessly in the grip of forces far stronger than human engineering.

"Both engines gone," MacReady announced in the sudden silence that followed the mechanical catastrophe. "She's dead in the water, Captain."

The words fell like a death sentence across the bridge. Without power, the Acadia was no longer a steamship but merely a floating box at the mercy of wind and wave.

Already she was beginning to drift, her bow falling off the wind as the gale took control of her destiny.

Captain Morrison stood frozen at the center of his bridge, staring at instruments that had suddenly become meaningless. The telegraph to the engine room no longer mattered when there were no engines to control. The compass was useless when the ship could no longer maintain course. Even the chronometer seemed to mock them, marking time toward a disaster that mechanical precision could not prevent.

"Sir?" The quartermaster's voice carried barely controlled panic. "Orders, sir?"

But Morrison had no orders to give. His entire career had been built on the assumption that steam power made seamanship secondary, that schedules and mechanical reliability could overcome any challenge the sea might present. Faced with the failure of that fundamental belief, he seemed paralyzed by the magnitude of his miscalculation.

It was Brennan who finally attempted to take charge, his voice sharp with the authority of a man refusing to acknowledge defeat. "Drop both anchors," he ordered. "We'll ride this out until the engines can be repaired."

But the anchors, designed for holding a steamship in harbor rather than against ocean gales, provided little security. The Acadia continued to drift, dragging her ground tackle through the sandy bottom as the storm drove her steadily toward the rocky coast that showed as an ominous line of white breakers through the darkness.

In the passenger saloon, panic was beginning to replace seasickness as word of their predicament spread. Families huddled together while businessmen demanded explanations that no one could provide. The comfortable certainty of steam travel had evaporated along with the pressure in the boilers, leaving only the ancient fear of humans confronting forces beyond their control.

"How far to shore?" one passenger demanded of Brennan during his inspection of the saloon.

"We're in no immediate danger," Brennan replied, but his voice lacked conviction. "The storm will moderate by morning, and repairs will be completed shortly thereafter."

Yet even as he spoke, everyone could feel the Acadia's continued drift toward the coast. Through the saloon windows, the occasional flash of lighthouse beam revealed a shoreline that seemed to grow closer with each passing hour. The anchors were holding them against the direct drive of the wind, but they could not prevent the inexorable sideways drift that was carrying the disabled steamship toward destruction.

On the bridge, Captain Morrison finally found his voice, though it carried none of its usual authority. "Signal for assistance," he ordered. "Fire distress rockets every fifteen minutes."

The rockets burst high overhead, their red stars brilliant against the storm clouds before being swallowed by the darkness. But what ships would be abroad in such weather? And even if help existed, could it reach them before the Acadia drove ashore on the unforgiving coast that lay somewhere ahead in the night?

As if in answer to these unspoken questions, a particularly violent gust of wind caught the steamship's superstructure, heeling her over until water sloshed across the main deck. When she rolled back upright, her drift toward shore had visibly increased, the anchors no longer able to hold against the combined force of wind and current.

"We're dragging faster," the quartermaster reported, his voice tight with fear. "At this rate, we'll be in the breakers before dawn."

Brennan turned on him savagely. "Hold your tongue! We'll maintain discipline aboard this vessel!"

But discipline meant nothing when the vessel herself was beyond human control. The Acadia continued her relentless drift toward shore, driven by forces that recognized no authority save their own. Steam power, which had promised mastery over the sea, had proven as fragile as human pride when tested against the storm's true strength.

In the engine room, MacReady and his men worked desperately to restore some measure of power, but the damage was too extensive for field repairs. Connecting rods lay twisted like broken bones, steam pipes leaked pressure faster than the boilers could generate it, and the intricate machinery that had once driven the paddle wheels now resembled the aftermath of an explosion.

"Nothing more we can do," MacReady finally admitted, his voice hollow with defeat. "Both engines are finished. Whatever happens now, it won't be steam power that saves us."

The admission echoed through the ship like a funeral bell, reaching every compartment where frightened passengers and crew waited for salvation that would not come from mechanical sources. The age of steam, which had promised such certainty and control, had failed them when they needed it most.

Outside, the storm raged on with undiminished fury, driving the helpless Acadia ever closer to the coast where breakers waited to complete the destruction that human hubris had begun. In a few hours, dawn would reveal how close they had drifted to disaster—and whether any power remained that might yet preserve them from the sea's final judgment.

Chapter 14: Canvas and Courage

Dawn broke gray and violent over a scene of maritime chaos. The Acadia lay wallowing in the storm swells less than two miles from a lee shore that showed white with breakers, her useless paddle wheels rising and falling with each wave like the wings of a dying bird. Through the spray and spindrift, the rocky coast of Nova Scotia loomed with pitiless clarity—close enough now that individual trees could be distinguished on the headlands, close enough that the sound of surf pounding against granite carried clearly across the water.

Captain Morrison stood on his bridge like a man attending his own execution, watching helplessly as wind and current drove his command toward destruction. The distress rockets fired throughout the night had brought no response; no rescue vessel would dare approach such a dangerous lee shore in these conditions. The Acadia's fate would be decided in the next few hours, and steam power could offer no salvation.

"How long before we strike?" Morrison asked the quartermaster, his voice barely audible above the wind.

"At this drift rate, sir... perhaps two hours. Maybe less if the wind increases."

Two hours. In two hours, the comfortable passenger steamer would become another wreck on Nova Scotia's unforgiving coast, her mechanical precision reduced to twisted metal and splintered wood. The passengers huddled in the saloon below knew it too; their earlier confidence in steam technology had given way to the kind of primal terror that no amount of modern engineering could dispel.

It was then that Elias Johnson stepped forward from his position at the back of the bridge, where he had stood silent through the long night of crisis. His voice, when he spoke, carried the quiet authority of a man who had faced such moments before and survived.

"Captain Morrison, I believe we can get her off this lee shore."

Morrison turned, his face showing a mixture of desperation and skepticism. "The engines are finished, Johnson. We have no power."

"No steam power," Elias corrected. "But she still has masts, and there's canvas in the sail locker—emergency storm sails that every steamship carries but rarely uses. With the wind where it is, we can rig enough sail to give her steerageway and work her clear of the coast."

Brennan's response was immediate and contemptuous. "Sails? On a steamship? That's the most ridiculous—"

"It's our only chance," Elias interrupted, his voice cutting through Brennan's objection with quiet certainty. "I've studied this vessel's rigging during the past weeks. She has a foremast and mainmast capable of carrying sail, and the wind is strong enough to drive her if we can get canvas on her."

Morrison's eyes showed the first glimmer of hope they had held since the engines failed. "You're certain this can be done?"

"I'm certain it's worth attempting, sir. The alternative is to drive ashore within the hour."

The captain's decision took only seconds. "Do it, Johnson. Take whoever you need and get sail on this ship."

Brennan's face flushed with rage. "Sir, I must protest! This man nearly destroyed our boilers through incompetence. You can't seriously consider—"

"I can and I will," Morrison snapped, his voice carrying the authority of command for the first time since the crisis began. "Mr. Johnson, you have full authority to rig whatever sail you think necessary. Mr. Brennan, you will assist in any way he requires."

The transformation in Elias was immediate and startling. The defeated subordinate who had endured weeks of systematic humiliation vanished, replaced by the master mariner who had commanded the Intrepid through countless gales. His movements became crisp and purposeful as he began issuing orders with the calm precision of a man in his element.

"Mr. MacReady, I need every available hand on deck. Passengers to remain below—this will be dangerous work.

Bosun Murphy, break out the emergency storm sails from the forward locker and prepare to rig running tackle to the foremast."

The crew responded with the desperate energy of men who suddenly saw salvation where moments before there had been only death. They scrambled across the spray-swept deck, fighting the ship's violent motion as they dragged canvas and cordage from storage compartments that had been sealed since the Acadia's construction.

The emergency sails were crude affairs compared to the finely cut canvas of a proper sailing ship—heavy, awkward triangular pieces meant only to provide minimal propulsion in extreme circumstances. But in Elias's hands, they became instruments of salvation as he calculated wind angles and sail trim with the expertise that had made him one of the finest sailing masters in the Maritime provinces.

"Rig the foresail first," he called to the men struggling with the unwieldy canvas. "Keep it reefed until we see how she handles. Santos, remember how we used to set storm canvas on the Providence? Same principles here."

Santos, the Portuguese rigger who had somehow found his way aboard the Acadia as an ordinary seaman, grinned through the spray as he attacked the rigging with renewed purpose. "Aye, Captain! Just like old times!"

The word "Captain" rippled through the crew like electricity. Here was a man who knew what he was about, who spoke their language and understood their craft. The mechanical mysteries of steam power meant nothing now; this was the ancient art of making sail work with wind and sea, and Elias Johnson was a master of that art.

But rigging sail on a steamship in a full gale proved more challenging than anyone had anticipated. The Acadia's masts were designed to support signal flags and wireless aerials, not the tremendous loads imposed by storm canvas. Every piece of running rigging had to be improvised from deck gear and cargo tackle, while the crew worked in constant danger of being swept overboard by the seas that crashed over the rail.

"Ease that halyard!" Elias shouted as the foresail began to take shape. "Don't fight the wind—work with it! Let her fill gradually or she'll tear herself apart!"

Brennan, reduced to the role of reluctant assistant, watched with growing amazement as his former captain transformed chaos into purpose. The man he had systematically humiliated was revealing skills that no amount of mechanical knowledge could replace—an intuitive understanding of how wind and canvas and cordage worked together to create motion from apparent chaos.

The foresail, when it finally set properly, had an immediate effect on the Acadia's behavior. Her bow began to pay off from the wind, giving her steerage way for the first time since the engines failed. But one sail was not enough; they needed more canvas to work clear of the threatening shore.

"Main storm trysail next," Elias ordered, his voice carrying clearly despite the wind. "Rig it as a jib—we need to balance her helm and give her more drive."

The second sail proved even more difficult to set. The improvised rigging stretched and strained under loads it was never designed to bear, while the crew fought to control canvas that wanted to tear itself from their hands. Twice the sail blew out of control, threatening to drag men overboard before they could regain command of it.

But gradually, piece by piece, Elias coaxed his makeshift rig into functional order. The Acadia began to move through the water with purpose rather than merely drifting at the wind's mercy. Her head came up, pointing away from the lee shore that had seemed certain doom only an hour before.

"She's making way!" the quartermaster called out, his voice cracking with emotion. "Two knots, maybe three!"

It was pitiful speed compared to the Acadia's normal cruising pace, but it was enough. Slowly, painfully, the steamship began to claw her way off the dangerous shore, each mile of sea room bought with the ancient skills that steam power had supposedly made obsolete.

Captain Morrison stood transfixed as he watched his ship transformed from helpless derelict to sailing vessel under Elias's guidance. The man he had demoted after the boiler incident was revealing capabilities that no amount of mechanical training could provide—the ability to read wind and weather, to understand how forces worked together, to improvise solutions when standard procedures failed.

"How did you know?" Morrison asked during a brief lull in the work. "How did you know this would work?"

Elias wiped spray from his face, his eyes never leaving the straining canvas. "Every ship wants to sail, Captain. Steam or sail, they're all built to move through water. You just have to understand what she needs and give it to her."

By noon, the immediate crisis had passed. The Acadia wallowed along under her jury rig at barely four knots, but she was making steady progress away from the coast. The storm continued to rage, but they now had sea room to maneuver, time to assess damage and plan their next move.

In the passenger saloon, word of their salvation had spread with the speed of wildfire. The same travelers who had scorned traditional seamanship now looked upon Elias with something approaching awe. He had literally snatched them from the jaws of death using skills they had assumed were as obsolete as wooden ships and iron men.

"Remarkable," commented Mr. Patterson, the textile manufacturer. "Who would have thought that old sailing techniques could save a modern steamship?"

But it was MacReady who perhaps understood best what had happened. "It wasn't technique," he told anyone who would listen. "It was seamanship—the real thing, not just following procedures. That man read the wind and sea like a book, then made this ship do what she needed to do to survive."

As the afternoon wore on and the Acadia continued her painful progress under improvised sail, the full magnitude of what Elias had accomplished became clear. He had not merely saved the ship; he had vindicated everything that traditional seamanship represented. In an age that had declared such skills obsolete, he had proven that understanding the sea was more valuable than understanding machines.

Brennan, forced to work alongside the man he had tormented, found his worldview crumbling with each successful maneuver. The engine room failures that had seemed to prove steam's superiority now revealed its fundamental weakness—when the machines failed, only human skill and courage could bridge the gap between civilization and disaster.

"How long can we maintain this?" Brennan asked grudgingly as they adjusted the set of the makeshift jib.

"As long as necessary," Elias replied simply. "The wind's moderating, and we're well clear of the shore now. We can work toward Halifax under sail, or wait for a tow if one becomes available."

"Under sail. In a steamship."

"Under sail," Elias confirmed. "The way ships moved for thousands of years before anyone dreamed of putting an engine in them."

As evening approached and the storm finally began to moderate, the Acadia continued her unlikely voyage under canvas. She was no longer the proud steamship that had departed Saint John on schedule, but she was alive and moving and carrying her passengers safely through waters that had nearly claimed them all.

On the bridge, Captain Morrison watched his unconventional command with growing respect for the man who had saved them. The mechanical precision of steam had failed when it was most needed, but the ancient art of seamanship had proven as reliable as the tide.

"Thank you, Johnson," Morrison said quietly. "I owe you an apology. We all do."

Elias nodded acknowledgment but kept his attention on the sails and the sea. There would be time for apologies later. For now, he was simply doing what he had always done—matching human skill against the sea's challenge and finding a way to prevail.

Behind them, the dangerous shore had faded into the distance. Ahead lay open water and the promise of safe harbor. The Acadia sailed on through the dying storm, her improvised rig a testament to the truth that seamanship, like the sea itself, was eternal.

Chapter 15: New Horizons

Three days after the storm, the Acadia limped into Halifax harbor under tow from the salvage tug Resolution, her improvised sails furled but her jury rig still standing as testament to the seamanship that had saved her. Word of the rescue had preceded them, carried by wireless messages and fishing boats that had witnessed the extraordinary sight of a steamship under sail fighting her way clear of a lee shore.

The waterfront was crowded with spectators as the disabled vessel was warped alongside the repair wharf. Maritime men who had spent their lives at sea stood in respectful silence, understanding better than landsmen what they were witnessing. Here was proof that the ancient skills of their fathers and grandfathers retained their value even in an age of mechanical marvels.

Elias stood on the Acadia's bridge, watching the familiar harbor close around them with mixed emotions. The past three days had vindicated everything he believed about seamanship, but they had also shown him how far the maritime world had traveled from its traditional roots. The passengers who thanked him so effusively for saving their lives would board the next steamer without a second thought, trusting their safety to mechanical systems that could fail as completely as the Acadia's engines had failed.

"Quite a homecoming," Captain Morrison observed, joining him at the rail. "The Marine Superintendent wants a full report, of course. There will be questions about our... unconventional navigation methods."

Morrison's tone had changed completely since the crisis. Gone was the patronizing dismissal of traditional seamanship, replaced by genuine respect for skills he had learned to value too late. The storm had taught him that commanding a steamship required more than understanding schedules and mechanical systems—it demanded the kind of sea sense that no amount of technical training could provide.

"I'll take full responsibility for the decision to rig sail," Morrison continued. "It was my choice to follow your recommendations."

"Our choice," Elias corrected. "And the right one."

Below them on the dock, Brennan supervised the disembarkation of passengers, his manner subdued but still carrying an edge of barely controlled resentment. The man who had spent weeks systematically humiliating his former captain now moved with the careful precision of someone whose fundamental assumptions had been challenged, but whose nature remained unchanged. When their eyes met briefly across the deck, Brennan's expression showed recognition of what had transpired— and hatred of the debt he now owed.

The formal inquiry took most of the following day. Captain Morrison presented his report to the Marine Superintendent and a panel of senior officers, describing the engine failures and the subsequent decision to rig emergency sail. His account was factual and thorough, giving full credit to Elias for both the idea and its execution.

"Irregular procedure," the Superintendent noted, reviewing Morrison's written report. "But effective under the circumstances. Mr. Johnson's actions undoubtedly saved the vessel and all aboard."

The vindication felt hollow to Elias. Official recognition of his seamanship was gratifying, but it didn't change the fundamental reality of his situation. Atlantic Steam had made it clear that his position aboard the Acadia was temporary—once the vessel was repaired, a new second officer would be assigned. His brief moment of heroism had earned respect but not security.

That evening, as he sat in a Halifax tavern nursing a pint and contemplating his uncertain future, a well-dressed stranger approached his table. The man was perhaps sixty, with the weathered complexion of someone who had spent considerable time at sea, though his expensive suit suggested current prosperity.

"Captain Johnson? Forgive the intrusion, but I believe we have business to discuss. John Willis of London—perhaps you know the name?"

Elias certainly knew the name. Jock Willis & Sons was one of the most prestigious shipping firms in the British Empire, owners of some of the finest sailing ships afloat.

Their clippers were legends in maritime circles—fast, beautiful vessels that commanded the most lucrative trades still open to sail.

"Mr. Willis. An honor, sir. Please, join me."

Willis settled into the opposite chair with the easy confidence of a successful businessman. "I've been following the reports of your recent... adventure aboard the Acadia. Remarkable seamanship by all accounts. Exactly the kind of thinking we value in our captains."

"Thank you, sir. But I'm afraid I'm currently under contract to Atlantic Steam."

"Temporarily, from what I understand. And frankly, Captain Johnson, steam service seems a waste of your particular talents." Willis signaled for a whiskey. "Tell me, what do you know of the Australian wool trade?"

"Fast passages, premium cargo, demanding seamanship. The domain of the finest sailing ships and masters."

"Precisely. And increasingly profitable as Australian production expands. We've been fortunate to dominate much of that trade with vessels like the Cutty Sark and Thermopylae." Willis paused as his drink arrived. "But we're expanding our fleet. The Patriarch—do you know her?"

Elias nodded. The Patriarch was legendary among sailing men—a clipper built by the same yard that had produced the Cutty Sark, designed for speed and capable of passages that put steamships to shame on long-distance routes.

"Beautiful ship. Fast as anything afloat."

"And currently without a master. Captain Hendricks took ill in Sydney—lung fever. He's been invalided home, which leaves us in need of a captain who can handle her on the wool runs." Willis studied Elias carefully. "It's demanding work. Three to four voyages per year to Australia and back, carrying premium cargo that tolerates no delays. The competition is fierce—every passage is a race against ships like the Thermopylae."

The offer was beyond anything Elias had dared hope for. Command of one of the world's finest sailing ships, trading on routes where seamanship still mattered more than schedules, competing against the best captains and vessels in the merchant marine. It represented everything he had thought lost when Morrison & Company was sold to the steam interests.

"What would be the terms?"

"Salary to match what you earned commanding the Intrepid, plus percentage of profits on fast passages—our captains do very well when they beat the competition to market. The Patriarch is berthed in London, taking on stores for her next voyage to Sydney. If you're interested, you could take command within the month."

Willis reached into his coat and produced a packet of papers. "Vessel specifications, recent voyage records, crew lists. Study them tonight and give me your answer in the morning. But I should warn you—this isn't coastal steaming with regular schedules and predictable conditions. The Southern Ocean doesn't forgive mistakes, and our shareholders expect results."

After Willis left, Elias spread the papers across his table and studied them by lamplight. The Patriarch's specifications read like poetry to a sailing man—195 feet of sleek beauty, built for speed with the finest materials and craftsmanship. Her recent voyage records showed passages that rivaled anything achieved by steam on the Australian run, with profits that justified the owners' investment in maintaining the finest sailing ships afloat.

The crew lists included names he recognized— experienced hands who had served aboard the best clippers, men who understood that sailing at this level required skills and dedication that lesser vessels never demanded. To command such a ship and crew would be to practice seamanship at its highest level, matching human expertise against the most challenging waters on Earth.

But it would also mean leaving behind the familiar waters of home, trading in distant seas where a captain's decisions could mean the difference between profit and bankruptcy, success and disaster. The wool clippers operated on margins that demanded perfection—one slow passage, one navigational error, one failure of judgment could end both voyage and career.

The next morning found Elias at the harbor office where Willis was reviewing shipping schedules. The older man looked up expectantly as Elias approached.

"Well, Captain? Have you decided?"

"I have, sir. I accept command of the Patriarch."

Willis smiled and extended his hand. "Excellent. You'll want to be in London within a fortnight—the wool season waits for no one, and we have a schedule to maintain."

The following week passed in a blur of preparations and farewells. Elias settled his affairs with Atlantic Steam, receiving grudging acknowledgment from the Marine Superintendent that his services had been valuable, if unconventional. Captain Morrison offered genuine regret at losing him, while expressing hope that their paths might cross again in calmer circumstances.

Brennan's reaction was more complex. Their final encounter occurred as Elias was leaving the company offices after collecting his final pay. The First Officer emerged from the Marine Superintendent's office, saw Elias in the corridor, and stopped abruptly.

For a moment, the two men faced each other in silence. Brennan's expression showed a mixture of emotions— recognition of the debt he owed, resentment at owing it, and something that might have been grudging respect for the man who had saved his life despite every provocation.

"So you're leaving us," Brennan said finally.

"New command. Sailing ship."

"Of course. Back to your proper element." Brennan's voice carried its familiar edge, but without the vicious satisfaction that had characterized their earlier exchanges. "Well. Good sailing to you, Johnson."

It wasn't an apology—Brennan's nature wouldn't permit that—but it was acknowledgment of sorts. Elias nodded curtly and continued toward the exit, knowing they would likely never meet again.

The voyage to London aboard the mail steamer gave Elias time to study the Patriarch's records in detail and prepare for the challenges ahead. The Australian wool trade was unforgiving, demanding captains who could read weather patterns across vast ocean distances, handle ships in the notorious gales of the Southern Ocean, and arrive in London ahead of competitors whose cargoes might flood the market and destroy profits.

But it was also the last refuge of pure seamanship in an increasingly mechanized world. Here, wind and weather still mattered more than coal consumption and boiler pressure. Success depended on understanding the sea rather than mastering machines, on reading signs that no steam engineer would ever comprehend.

Standing on the steamer's deck as the Irish coast slid past, Elias reflected on the strange turns his career had taken. Six months ago, he had been a comfortable sailing master confident in his abilities and his future. The loss of that certainty had been painful, but it had led him to this moment—command of one of the world's finest sailing ships, trading on routes where his skills would be tested against the best masters and vessels afloat.

The Cutty Sark, Thermopylae, and their sister ships represented the pinnacle of sailing ship design and seamanship. To command the Patriarch was to join an elite fraternity of captains who understood that the sea remained unconquered, that success required more than following procedures or maintaining schedules.

In London, the Patriarch waited at her berth, her tall masts rising proudly above the forest of steamship funnels that dominated the modern harbor. She was beautiful in the way that only the finest sailing ships could be—purposeful, elegant, built for speed rather than mere utility. Her lines spoke of designers who understood that moving through water required harmony between human skill and natural forces.

Within days, Elias would take command and begin preparations for the long voyage to Australia. The Southern Ocean lay ahead, with its legendary gales and the kind of challenges that separated competent sailors from true masters. But he faced that prospect without fear, knowing that he was returning to his proper element—a world where seamanship still mattered, where experience and judgment could overcome any storm.

The age of sail was ending, but it was not yet finished. In ships like the Patriarch, crewed by men who understood

159

the sea's moods and mysteries, the ancient traditions would endure. They would race the wind across vast distances, carrying valuable cargoes between distant continents, proving that some things could not be replaced by mechanical convenience.

Behind him lay months of humiliation and defeat, the bitter lesson that the world was changing in ways that threatened everything he had worked to achieve. Ahead stretched new horizons where his skills would find their proper expression, where the partnership between sailor and sea continued to create something larger than either could achieve alone.

The Patriarch would be his command, but more than that, she would be his vindication—proof that seamanship was more than obsolete tradition, that understanding wind and wave remained as valuable as it had ever been. In her, he would find not just employment but purpose, carrying forward traditions that connected him to every master mariner who had ever matched skill against the sea's challenge.

London's harbor stretched before him, forest of masts and maze of waterways that had made Britain the maritime center of the world. Somewhere among those vessels, the Patriarch waited for her new captain, ready to prove once again that the finest sailing ships could still outrun steam and outclass anything that mechanical ingenuity had yet produced.

The future was no longer certain, but it was once again bright with possibility.

Chapter 16: The Green Flash

The London Docks at dawn were a marvel of controlled chaos, with ships from every corner of the Empire discharging their cargoes while others prepared for distant voyages. Steam and sail mingled in harmonious confusion —great paddle steamers shouldering alongside elegant clippers, their different purposes united by the common goal of moving the world's trade through Britain's maritime heart.

Elias made his way through the bustle toward the East India Dock, where Jock Willis had told him the Patriarch lay berthed. He carried his sea chest and navigational instruments, the tools of his trade that had served him faithfully through twenty-three years of professional seamanship. Today, they would find their proper home aboard one of the finest sailing ships ever built.

He saw her masts first, rising above the forest of rigging like cathedral spires, her yards crossed with mathematical precision. Then the Patriarch herself came into view, and Elias felt his breath catch. She was everything the specifications had promised and more—195 feet of purposeful beauty, her black hull gleaming with fresh paint, her copper sheathing bright as new pennies below the waterline.

The clipper sat in the water with the grace of a thoroughbred, her fine lines speaking of speed and the kind of engineering that married art with science. Her figurehead, a noble patriarch with flowing beard and commanding presence, gazed eastward toward the distant waters she was built to conquer. Everything about her suggested power held in restraint, waiting for wind and the touch of skilled hands to unleash her true potential.

"Captain Johnson, I presume?"

The voice belonged to a compact, weathered man in his forties who approached from the ship's gangway. His bearing and the careful way he studied Elias marked him as the kind of professional seaman who had spent his life aboard the finest vessels.

"I'm Thomas McKenzie, First Mate of the Patriarch. The lads are eager to meet their new skipper."

Elias shook the mate's hand, noting the callused palms and steady gaze of a man who understood his business. "Pleased to meet you, Mr. McKenzie. What's her condition?"

"Sound as a bell, sir. Mr. Willis spares no expense in her maintenance. We've just completed loading—finest Australian wool, bound for the mills of Yorkshire. Three hundred tons of premium cargo that the buyers are eager to receive."

They crossed the gangway together, and Elias felt the familiar sensation of a deck beneath his feet responding to his weight. The Patriarch's deck was immaculate—holystoned planking white as bone, brass fittings that gleamed like gold, rigging that spoke of constant attention and seamanlike pride.

"She's beautiful," Elias said, and meant it.

"Aye, sir. Built by Hercules Linton at Dumbarton—same yard that gave us the Cutty Sark. No finer builder of fast ships in all the world. The Patriarch's made some remarkable passages in her time."

As they toured the vessel, Elias found himself increasingly impressed by what Willis's money and careful attention had created. The crew quarters were spacious by clipper standards, the galley well-equipped, the sail locker stocked with canvas that represented the finest work of British sailmakers. Everything spoke of a ship maintained regardless of expense, fitted out for masters who understood that success in the competitive wool trade demanded perfection in every detail.

But it was the ship's lines that truly captured his imagination. Standing on her quarterdeck and looking forward along her length, Elias could see the mathematical precision that had gone into her design. Every curve served a purpose, every angle calculated to move through water with minimum resistance and maximum speed. She was a weapon in the war against time and distance, built for masters who understood that arriving first meant the difference between profit and loss.

"What's her best passage?" Elias asked as they completed their inspection.

"Sydney to London in seventy-six days, sir. Captain Hendricks drove her hard through some heavy weather in the Southern Ocean, but she responded like the thoroughbred she is. The Cutty Sark made it in seventy-three that same season, but only by a day when you account for different sailing dates."

Seventy-six days from Australia to London—a pace that would shame most steamships even allowing for their need to coal. It spoke of seamanship at its highest level, of a captain who could read weather patterns across vast ocean distances and drive his ship through conditions that would have destroyed lesser vessels.

The crew assembled on deck that afternoon for the traditional ceremony of reading the articles. Twenty-six men in all, from green hands seeking their first taste of deep water to veteran able seamen who had sailed aboard the finest clippers. Their faces showed the mixture of wariness and hope that always accompanied a change of command—uncertainty about their new captain's methods balanced against the promise of good wages and fast passages.

"Men," Elias began, his voice carrying clearly in the afternoon stillness, "we sail with tomorrow's tide for Sydney. This ship has a reputation for fast passages and profitable voyages. I intend to maintain both."

He paused, studying the faces before him. Some he recognized from their reputations—Santos the rigger had somehow found his way to London and a berth aboard the Patriarch, while others were new to him but carried themselves with the unmistakable bearing of professional seamen.

"I'll drive her hard when conditions warrant, but never beyond her limits or yours. Any man who can't accept that is free to leave now with his advance pay." He waited, but no one moved. "Very well. We'll work her as a team—ship, crew, and cargo together. Questions?"

A grizzled bosun stepped forward. "Will we be racing, sir? The Thermopylae sails next week with wool cargo, and there's talk she means to beat our time to London."

Elias smiled. "Mr. Peterson, every passage is a race when you're carrying premium cargo. But we'll sail our own race, not theirs. The Patriarch will show her heels to any ship afloat if we handle her properly."

The crew dispersed to their preparations with the kind of purposeful energy that marked a well-found ship preparing for sea. Elias remained on deck, familiarizing himself with every detail of his new command. The steering gear, compass, and deck layout were different from the Intrepid, but the fundamental principles remained constant. This was a sailing ship, designed to work in harmony with wind and weather rather than against them.

As evening approached, the last of their stores came aboard—fresh water, preserved provisions, and the thousand items necessary for a voyage that might last four months. The Patriarch settled slightly deeper into the Thames as her holds filled, but she retained the eager look of a ship straining to be gone.

That night, alone in his cabin, Elias spread his charts across the table and began planning their route to Sydney. The course would take them down the English Channel, across the Bay of Biscay, and then south along the African coast to the Cape of Good Hope. From there, the great circle route across the Indian Ocean to Australia, threading their way through some of the most challenging waters on Earth.

The Southern Ocean particularly demanded respect—the notorious "Roaring Forties" where westerly gales could drive a ship at speeds that would terrify steamship passengers, but where one mistake in navigation or sail handling could end in disaster. It was seamanship at its most demanding, requiring captains who could read weather signs days in advance and make split-second decisions that affected both cargo and crew.

The tide turned at four in the morning, and by dawn the Patriarch was warped out into the Thames, her sails bent and ready for sea. London's great port spread around them in magnificent confusion—merchant ships from every corner of the Empire, naval vessels maintaining Britain's maritime supremacy, and the countless smaller craft that served the world's busiest harbor.

"Single up all lines," Elias called as they approached the harbor mouth. "Prepare to make sail."

The crew moved with practiced efficiency, their months of working together evident in every coordinated movement. Gaskets came off the courses, topsails, and jibs while the yards were manned and ready. The Patriarch trembled slightly as the Thames current caught her, eager to feel wind in her sails.

"Let fall the fore and main courses! Sheet home and hoist away!"

Canvas tumbled from the yards and bellied out as the wind caught it, transforming the Patriarch from static object to living entity. She gathered way slowly at first, then with increasing purpose as more sail was set. The motion beneath Elias's feet changed from the dead response of a moored vessel to the live, eager movement of a ship finding her element.

"Set the topsails! Fore and main t'gallants!"

More canvas bloomed above them, and the Patriarch's speed increased noticeably. Her bow began to lift and fall with the rhythm that marked a ship moving in harmony with the sea, while spray started to fly from her cutwater in brilliant sheets that caught the morning sun.

They cleared the Thames estuary and shaped course for the Channel, the Patriarch settling into her stride with the satisfaction of a thoroughbred finding good footing. Her movement was unlike anything Elias had experienced aboard steamships—not the mechanical thrust of paddle wheels, but the complex interplay of hull, sails, and sea that created motion from natural forces.

By noon they were well into the Channel, the Patriarch logging eight knots in a moderate southwesterly breeze. Her behavior under sail was everything the specifications had promised—responsive to the helm, quick to answer changes in wind direction, capable of maintaining speed through the kind of variable conditions that plagued steamers.

"She's a beauty, sir," McKenzie observed, joining Elias on the quarterdeck. "Handles like a yacht but carries cargo like a merchant vessel. Mr. Willis chose well when he commissioned her."

The afternoon brought stronger winds and the opportunity to show what the Patriarch could truly accomplish. As the breeze freshened to force five, Elias ordered the skysails set—the highest canvas that only the finest ships could carry safely. The clipper responded with a surge of speed that pressed her lee rail down toward the water, sending spray flying in sheets that caught the light like jewels.

"Twelve knots, sir," the mate reported, his voice showing the excitement that fast sailing always generated among true seamen. "She's flying!"

As evening approached and they cleared the English coast, Elias found himself alone on the quarterdeck, watching the sun sink toward the western horizon. The Patriarch rushed through the darkening water with a sound like distant thunder, her wake stretching behind them in a perfectly straight line that spoke of skillful steering and balanced sail.

He thought of the strange journey that had brought him to this moment—from master of the Intrepid to disgraced second officer aboard a steamship, then finally to command of one of the world's finest sailing vessels. The humiliation aboard the Acadia seemed like something from another life, overcome by the vindication of this return to his proper element.

The sea had tested him in ways he never could have anticipated, stripping away the comfortable certainties of his earlier career and forcing him to confront the harsh realities of technological change. But it had also revealed truths about seamanship that no amount of mechanical innovation could alter—that understanding wind and weather remained as valuable as it had ever been, that the partnership between sailor and sea created something larger than either could achieve alone.

Behind them, the lights of England faded into the gathering dusk. Ahead lay Sydney and the challenging waters of the Southern Ocean, where the Patriarch would prove her worth against some of the finest ships and masters afloat. It would be seamanship at its most demanding, requiring everything Elias had learned during his years at sea.

But he faced that prospect without fear, knowing that he had found his proper place in a changing world. The age of sail might be ending, but it was not yet finished. In ships like the Patriarch, crewed by men who understood the sea's moods and mysteries, the ancient traditions would endure.

The sun touched the horizon, a crimson disk that painted the western sky in shades of gold and scarlet. As it sank toward the sea, Elias watched for the phenomenon that sailors had treasured for centuries—the green flash that sometimes appeared at the moment of sunset, visible only to those whose eyes were trained to read the sea's subtle signs.

"Set the royals," he called to the watch. "We'll carry everything she'll take."

The highest sails unfurled in the dying light, adding their power to the Patriarch's already impressive speed. She surged forward with renewed purpose, her tall masts swaying against the star-filled sky as she found her rhythm for the long voyage ahead.

And then, as the sun's last rim disappeared beneath the horizon, it came—a brilliant flash of emerald light that lasted only seconds but seemed to illuminate the entire world. The green flash, rarest of maritime phenomena, visible only in perfect conditions to those who knew how to look for it.

Elias smiled as the light faded, taking it as an omen of fair winds and successful passages ahead. The Patriarch rushed on through the darkness, carrying him toward waters where his skills would find their ultimate expression, where the partnership between sailor and sea continued to create something beautiful and eternal.

The green flash was gone, but its promise remained—that some things transcended the mechanical certainties of the modern world, that mystery and wonder still existed for those brave enough to seek them on the vast waters that covered most of the Earth.

Ahead lay adventure, challenge, and the kind of sailing that made all the struggles worthwhile. Behind them, England's lights disappeared into the night, but the future stretched bright with possibility across the dark waters of the Atlantic.

Back Matter

Historical Note

The transition from sail to steam in the 1870s represented one of the most dramatic technological shifts in maritime history. Within a single generation, skills that had been refined over centuries became obsolete on many trade routes, while entirely new forms of seamanship emerged around mechanical propulsion.

The Maritime provinces of Canada were particularly affected by this change. Communities like Yarmouth, Halifax, and Saint John had built their prosperity on wooden ships and iron men, producing some of the finest sailing vessels and most skilled mariners in the world. The Golden Age of Sail reached its peak in the 1860s and 1870s, just as steam technology was making these achievements irrelevant.

The Ships:

- The **Cutty Sark** (1869) was indeed one of the fastest tea clippers ever built, later becoming famous in the Australian wool trade
- The **Thermopylae** (1868) was her greatest rival, and their legendary races captured public imagination

- The **Patriarch** (1869) was a real clipper owned by Jock Willis & Sons, built by the same yard as Cutty Sark
- Morrison & Company represents the many Maritime shipping firms that were absorbed by larger steam companies during this period

The Transition: By 1880, steam had captured most passenger routes and mail services. Sailing ships survived longest in bulk cargo trades where speed was less critical than economy. The last commercial sailing ships carrying cargo disappeared in the 1920s and 1930s, though a few continued in specialized roles into the 1950s.

Many experienced sailing ship officers did adapt to steam service, often starting at reduced ranks. Others found employment with the remaining sailing vessel operators or left the sea entirely. The human cost of this technological revolution was significant, though rarely recorded in official histories.

Maritime Culture: The Maritime provinces maintained their connection to traditional seamanship longer than most regions, with sailing vessels continuing to operate from smaller ports well into the 20th century. The skills and values developed during the Age of Sail—self-reliance, craftsmanship, and intimate knowledge of wind and weather—became part of the regional character that persists today.

Glossary of Nautical Terms

Barque/Bark: Three-masted vessel, square-rigged on fore and main masts, fore-and-aft rigged on mizzen

Brigantine: Two-masted vessel, square-rigged on foremast, fore-and-aft rigged on mainmast

Clipper: Fast sailing ship designed for speed rather than cargo capacity, typically used in premium trades

Course: The largest sail on each mast, set on the lowest yard

Dead Reckoning: Navigation by calculating position based on speed, time, and direction from a known starting point

Fore-and-aft Rigged: Sails set parallel to the ship's centerline (like modern sailboats)

Jury Rig: Temporary rigging or sails improvised to replace damaged equipment

Lee Shore: Coast toward which the wind is blowing— dangerous for sailing ships

Packet: Vessel running regular scheduled service between specific ports

Square-rigged: Sails set perpendicular to the ship's centerline on horizontal yards

Topsail: Sail set above the course on each mast

Trysail: Small triangular sail used in heavy weather

Windward: Direction from which the wind is blowing

Bibliography

Primary Sources:

- Ships' logs and crew lists, Maritime Museum of the Atlantic
- *The Halifax Chronicle* and *Yarmouth Herald*, 1870-1880
- Lloyd's Register of Shipping, 1870-1890
- Parliamentary Papers on Steam Navigation, British House of Commons

Secondary Sources:

- Armour, Charles A. *Sailing Ships of the Maritimes*. Toronto: McGraw-Hill Ryerson, 1975.
- Lubbock, Basil. *The Colonial Clippers*. Glasgow: Brown, Son & Ferguson, 1921.
- MacNutt, W.S. *The Atlantic Provinces: The Emergence of Colonial Society*. Toronto: McClelland & Stewart, 1965.
- Sager, Eric W. *Seafaring Labour: The Merchant Marine of Atlantic Canada*. Montreal: McGill-Queen's University Press, 1989.

Author's Note

Dead Reckoning is set during the 1870s, a pivotal decade in maritime history when steam power was rapidly displacing sail in commercial shipping. While the characters and specific events in this novel are fictional, the historical context is authentic—based on extensive research into the Maritime provinces' shipping industry, the transition from sail to steam, and the experiences of professional mariners during this period of technological revolution.

The ships mentioned—including the famous clippers Cutty Sark, Thermopylae, and Patriarch—were real vessels that competed in the lucrative trades described in these pages. The technical details of seamanship, navigation, and ship handling reflect the actual practices of the era, drawn from period sources including ships' logs, maritime newspapers, and the memoirs of captains who lived through this transformation.

Special acknowledgment goes to the Maritime Museum of the Atlantic, the National Maritime Museum in Greenwich, and the archives of Lloyd's Register, whose collections preserve the records of ships and sailors from this remarkable period in maritime history.

For the mariners of Nova Scotia, who carried the traditions of the sea through changing times

Acknowledgments

The author wishes to thank the staff of the Maritime Museum of the Atlantic in Halifax, whose collections and expertise made this novel possible. Special gratitude to the archivists who preserve the records of ships and sailors from this remarkable period.

Thanks also to the working sail training ships that keep traditional seamanship alive, allowing modern observers to understand what sailing a square-rigged vessel actually entailed. The experience of watching professional mariners handle traditional sailing ships provides insights that no amount of reading can match.

Finally, appreciation to the descendants of Maritime shipping families, who have preserved family papers, photographs, and stories that illuminate the human side of this technological revolution.

About the Author

Del Wilber is a decorated Navy veteran with a distinguished 20-year career flying the mighty P-3 Orion aircraft as a Aircrewman. He is an autodidact who went on to earn a BS in General Science from Excelsior University, an M.Ed. In Instructional Design from AIU, and a Ph.D. in Education from Capella University. He has also completed many courses from Walden University and Texas A&M. He taught himself to play guitar and learn how to sail. He is an accomplished sailor who prefers single-handed ocean passages and has owned many sailboats. He lives the quiet life at home with his wife, his dog, and a parrot who talks too much.

For more information about Maritime history and the Age of Sail, visit:

- Maritime Museum of the Atlantic, Halifax, Nova Scotia
- National Maritime Museum, Greenwich, England
- Mystic Seaport Museum, Mystic, Connecticut

www.ingramcontent.com/pod-product-compliance
Lightning Source LLC
Chambersburg PA
CBHW051124260626
47170CB00005B/1649